The SPY Wore SHADES

by
MARTHA FREEMAN

HarperCollinsPublishers

The author thanks caver and naturalist Keith Christenson for his gracious help and invaluable expertise. Several other people also helped enormously with this manuscript, including Jane Jordan Browne and Janie McAdams, Meredith Charpentier, Bob Benson and Barbara French of Bat Conservation International, Dr. Richard Cunningham, Chris Bateman, Ela Sikora, and Rosa Frank.

The Spy Wore Shades

www.harperchildrens.com

Library of Congress Cataloging-in-Publication Data
Freeman, Martha, date.
  The spy wore shades / by Martha Freeman.
    p.   cm.
  Summary: Eleven-year-old Dougie, living in California's Calaveras County, teams up with twelve-year-old Varloo, an emissary from a culture living in underground caves, and tries to help her people.
  ISBN 0-06-029269-5 — ISBN 0-06-029270-9 (lib. bdg.)
    [1. Caves—California—Fiction. 2. Druids and Druidism—Fiction. 3. Friendship—Fiction. 4. California—Fiction.] I. Title.
PZ7.F87496 Sp 2001   00-59704
[Fic]—dc21   CIP
                                                              AC

Typography by Andrea Simkowski

1 3 5 7 9 10 8 6 4 2
❖
First Edition

For Russell, our household poet,
who gave me the title and a lot more.
And for Sylvie, our aspiring singer
and songwriter.

Chapter One

A Sunday afternoon in October

"**M**R. JETT! MR. JETT! OVER HERE!"

Dougie Minners stood in a crush of happy, jostling fans outside the players' entrance at the Coliseum in Oakland, California. Only a little while before, the Oakland Raiders had come back to beat New York in the final seconds of the game. Oakland—perennial misfits of the NFL—had suffered two humiliating losses in two weeks. The fans were thrilled to have something to celebrate.

Dougie Minners had a second reason to be happy. His dad and his little brother, Judah, had wanted to leave in the third quarter when the Raiders were down by seventeen points; Dougie had talked them out of it.

"You know what Mom says," he had told them. "Where there's life, there's hope!"

Judah howled in protest. Dad rolled his eyes. But in the end they stayed, and the game turned out to be not only a win but an exciting one. Dougie liked being right about something. It didn't happen that often.

Now the appearance of wide receiver James Jett in the doorway caused Dougie and the rest of the waiting Raider faithful to whoop and holler. Without the uniform padding Jett seemed pretty normal size, Dougie thought. Not like a hero at all. Still, he was one.

It was Jett who had slipped past two defenders and caught Rich Gannon's pass in the end zone, tying the score with twenty-six seconds left in the game. At first nobody in the Coliseum had believed it, not even the ref, who hesitated before raising his arms to signal the touchdown. When he did, the crowd erupted. Placekicker Michael Husted made the point after, and the Raiders pulled a victory out of a mess, 24–23.

"Mr. Jett! Mr. Jett!" Dougie yelled, and waved his pen. He had never seen a football game in person before, and Dad had bought him a Raider ball cap as a souvenir. If James Jett would sign that hat . . .

"Come on, Dougie. Let's go." Judah Minners, Dougie's little brother, tugged on his jacket. "It's a long drive home, and we've got school tomorrow. I want to get to bed on time."

That's a 49er fan for you, Dougie thought. The most thrilling Raider game in years, and Judah's thinking about bedtime.

"Hang on, buddy," Dad said to Judah. "We can wait a few more minutes."

James Jett smiled at his fans. "Thanks, folks. The win feels real good. But no autographs today. Sorry."

Dougie groaned along with the rest of the crowd as Jett waved and made his way toward the players' parking lot. Most people turned back to the doorway then, hoping Rich Gannon would appear soon. But Dougie kept his eyes on Jett, and miraculously Jett glanced over at him. Dougie would never know why it happened exactly. Later he thought it might have been the tragic expression on his face. Whatever it was, James Jett flashed him a big grin and said, "Okay, kid. Just one autograph today. Give me that hat."

It was the happiest moment in Dougie Minners's life.

Chapter Two

A Saturday evening the following May

THEY COULDN'T FIND VARLOO'S HAT. Varloo was sure she had hung it on the knob by the flap, but her mother said it was not there now, and the Druids would be gathered at the Portal by the time of the awakening. Surely Varloo did not intend to keep the Druids waiting?

"No," said Varloo. Even she was a little afraid of the Druids. "But I dare not depart without it, Mother."

Persephone put her own hat on Varloo's head. "'Tis overlarge, but 'twill suffice. Mayhap Osi will lead you to another on your Mission."

"'Tis permitted? To take a hat from the Extros?"

"Varloo." Her mother knelt down and looked into her pale blue eyes. "You have studied the Story, and you know well the Song of the Hero. As long as you do not consort yourself with them, you may take what you will."

"Aye, Mother," Varloo said quickly. "'Tis only that I am a mite anxious. I know what is permitted."

Persephone shook her head, then closed her eyes for a moment. "Varloo," she finally said, "your grandmother, your tutors, all of us have done what we can do. Now the responsibility belongs to you. You have only attained the age of twelve. This makes you—"

"—the youngest Spy in the history of Hek." Varloo had heard this so often she repeated it out of habit.

"You must needs remember your lessons," said her mother. "You must needs remember that you are the first daughter of the first daughter, and the daughter of a Druid."

Varloo tried not to let exasperation steal into her voice. "Aye, Mother."

"You have the rucksack? The map? The shaded spectacles?"

"Aye, Mother."

"The lead for Osi?"

Varloo nodded. "Uh . . . Mother? May I not have one more mushroom cake? They are so savory, and my journey may be long."

Persephone shook her head. "No, my daughter. You have eaten three. Even your father, may he sleep peacefully, never ate so many at once."

Varloo frowned. Her father was often held up to her as a model of right behavior. Besides enjoying a healthful appetite, he had been a Druid and a member of the Council, admired by nearly everyone in Hek. But in spite of the finest elixirs the alchemists could devise, he had sickened and died when Varloo was still a baby. All she knew of him were the songs her mother and grandmother sang.

"Let us make haste now." Mother pushed open the flap, and the two walked out of the dwelling place and down the Southwest Passageway. Just before the tunnel turned, Varloo looked back at the flap, its gold border shining in the lantern light. Unbidden, a question came to her mind: Shall I ever see it again?

She tried to banish the foolish thought with a shake of her head, which made her mother's big hat slip down over her eyes. Blind for a moment, Varloo stumbled and caught hold of a stalagmite to right herself.

Of course I shall see it again, she reassured herself. Only five sleeps from now.

They crossed the Park. In the distance Varloo observed a sentry on his rounds. It was too early for anyone else to be about; besides, the rules of the departure ceremony forbade any but her mother, the principal Bard, and the Druids to be in attendance. Varloo thought she would have liked it if some of her near age-mates could be there to see. Wouldn't they be impressed to see her at last wearing the robe of the Spy? The gold necklace? To see her take charge of the sacred cat?

Varloo and her mother reached the South Stairs and began the ascent. Halfway up she stopped to rest, but her mother hurried her forward toward the South Portal Tunnel. Varloo was breathing hard as they walked beneath the Vent, a small opening to the Surface where the string of lanterns was interrupted and a few straggly ferns grew wild.

"Whence comes the light?" Varloo asked. "'Tis nearly the time of sleep for the Extros." She wanted her mother to know she remembered something.

But a pained expression crossed Persephone's face. "You have forgotten the full moon."

"The full moon," Varloo repeated. The *moon* was the orb that lit the ceiling—that is, the *sky*. She didn't remember what it meant that it should be *full*. Who could pay attention to so many details, so many lessons? Lectured by her tutors in the Great Hall, Varloo had preferred to watch the bats flitting overhead.

At the intersection with the North Passageway Varloo saw the glint of gold in the purple robes of the Druids, who were moving ahead of them toward the Portal. The departure ceremony was to be brief, her mother had promised. Geber would utter ritual words about the significance of the Mission, Varloo would reply, her mother would clasp about her neck the gold necklace, emblem of the Spy, and Geber would hand her Osi. Then someone would pull the lever, and the forbidden staircase would descend.

Simple.

Except that it was not. When the moment came, Varloo did not remember the words of the reply to Geber's declaration. Instead she stammered something all wrong about what a fine job she would do. Geber's eyes grew angry at the breach of tradition, and Varloo heard a murmur among the other members of the Council. But Varloo stood fast and held Geber's gaze. He might be a Druid and the senior member of the Council, but he would not dare to interfere with her Mission.

Then there was the necklace. Persephone's hands shook so that she nearly dropped it. And Osi, the sacred cat, was especially ill-tempered; she hissed when she was placed in Varloo's arms.

Varloo could not fail to notice how inauspicious were the omens. Perhaps it was well that none of her near age-mates was there to see.

Varloo's grandmother, herself a Druid, interrupted her thoughts. "The lever, child."

"Aye, Grandmother." Clutching Osi in one arm, Varloo turned and grasped the shiny silver handle on the rock wall behind her. Then she hesitated. Even though she had been told to do so, it felt so odd to violate a Tenet.

"Varloo—," Geber began. He was losing patience.

Without waiting to hear more, Varloo pulled. The whir of the stairs descending was followed by the squeal of old metal complaining. Restless, Osi meowed in response. Finally gears began to hum, and for the first time in half a century the staircase descended from the ceiling. The bottom step touched down inches from Varloo's feet. She looked up into a beam of light from the—what had her mother called it? *Full moon?*

"Fare thee well, Varloo," said her grandmother. Her kiss was warm on Varloo's cheek. But on her face was the same troubled expression Varloo had seen on her mother's. Varloo then allowed the Bard and each of the other Druids to kiss her—even

Geber. When it was her mother's turn, she saw tears in her eyes. So that she would not cry herself, Varloo turned away quickly and placed the big gray cat on the stairs.

"Proceed, Osi," she said. Osi stretched, in no hurry to be off, and raised her nose to sniff the unfamiliar air from the world above. "You may proceed, Osi," Varloo said. She wanted this departure over and done with, and when Osi sat down and began washing her face, she bumped the cat's rump with her toe, hoping no one would notice.

"The Spy does kick the sacred cat!" Geber cried in disbelief, but his voice was drowned out by Osi's own protest: *"Rrrrreeeeeooowwwwww!"*

Varloo's tactic may have dismayed Geber, but it was effective. The cat leaped ahead on the staircase. Varloo, one hand keeping the floppy hat in place, trotted along behind.

A few seconds later, breathing hard, she crawled beneath the Portal boulder and into the blinding moonlight of the Extros' world. Almost immediately she heard the clatter and squeal of the staircase rising, cutting off access to her home. Over the noise her mother's voice barely reached her: "Don the shaded spectacles!"

10

Chapter Three

Later the same night

THE THIRD TIME MOM told him to turn off his light and go to sleep, Dougie looked up from his book. "What, Mom?"

She was standing by his bed. "It's eleven o'clock!"

Dougie shook his head. Didn't Mom understand anything? The three-toed moon worms were about to perform the lava experiment. He couldn't possibly go to sleep without knowing if all the earthlings were burned up.

"What are you doing awake anyway?" Dougie asked.

"Working," she said. "As always. That Spook Hill project seems to eat all my time."

Dougie didn't know what the Spook Hill project was, but he nodded as if he did. "Just a few more minutes?" he begged.

"How many more pages?"

"Hardly any," Dougie said. "Maybe a hundred."

"Dougie! We're going to church in the morning."

"Okay, okay." Dougie made a show of yawning, pulling the covers up, and turning out his light.

Mom smiled and came over to kiss him. "We need to leave by nine," she said. "You're coming, aren't you?"

Dougie wasn't planning to. But this was not the time to argue. "Mmm-huh," he mumbled.

"Mmm-huh yourself," Mom said. Then she closed his door.

Dougie rolled onto his back and thought about moon worms while he stared at the stick-on planets that glowed on his ceiling. Soon the house was quiet. Dougie counted to twenty. Then he turned his light on and reached for his book.

Chapter Four

Seven spies before me stood
'Neath the spreading, sacred oak,
Did look to sky as I now look
And thought of home that lies below.
From the *Song of Varloo*, Sleep One

VARLOO'S FIRST IMPRESSION of the Extros' world was a bright blur, painful to her eyes. And poor Osi actually walked into the Portal rock, batted it, and hissed. The cat must have thought the rock was attacking her.

"Now where are they?" Varloo muttered. She untied the flap of her rucksack and rifled through it, among food packets, matches, her folded shelter, and her clothing, before remembering that she had put the shaded spectacles in a side pocket so they would be easy to find. Once the dark lenses were over her eyes, she could see her surroundings.

What struck her first was that amazing bright orb on the ceiling—that is, the *full moon* in the *sky*, she reminded herself—and all the tiny dots of light that surrounded it. *Stars*. Then there was the sheer size of the black dome that stretched away from her endlessly, so different from the cozy closeness of the rock ceiling at home. Other Spies had mentioned this in their songs, of course. But it was one thing to hear about, quite another to experience, such vastness. Varloo did not like to feel so small.

She wondered momentarily what the day would be like, when that even brighter orb called *sun* turned the sky a fearsome blue.

Varloo focused next on those things that were nearer to hand. According to the Story, the Portal, marked by the white boulder, was located on a hillside below an ancient oak tree. Varloo turned to look up the hill and there saw the tree. Hung abundantly with mistletoe, it looked comfortingly familiar: Its image adorned the Hekian flag, the flaps of many dwelling places, the walls of the Great Hall.

More than four hundred years before, the same oak had been the sign that told the first Hekians, those who came from across the water, that this was the haven they sought. Odin had directed the men to shift the boulder, and beneath it the Portal to the underground caverns had been revealed.

"Osi?" Varloo looked down and saw that the cat also surveyed their surroundings. "Strange, is it not?" The very air was odd, so sharp and dry it stung Varloo's nose, nothing like the pleasant moist mustiness of the air at home.

It was cold too. She had learned that the Extros endured something called *seasons*, varying hours of light and darkness, varying temperatures. It seemed like such an unsettled way to live! Varloo thought how very superior was the constant temperance in the caverns of Hek.

But this was no time to dwell on her home. Varloo had work to do. She needed a site on which to construct her shelter. It must be completed before daybreak so that she might have refuge from the light.

There were none of the telltale signs of Extros near to the Portal, so Varloo decided she should journey nearer to the settlement described by her grandmother, Brigid, the previous Spy. Varloo removed the map from her rucksack and consulted it. The creek was . . . let's see . . . behind her, and the settlement would be beyond that. But wait— that did not make sense. The creek could not be uphill, could it? Varloo turned the map around. Now it looked as though the creek was below her. She tried turning the map sideways. Downhill, she decided. Anyway, it was easier to walk downhill. The climb up the staircase had tired her.

"Come along, Osi." Varloo took a few steps and looked back. Osi had not moved.

"O my Drake," Varloo said. "I am five minutes into my Mission, and already I am suffering a crisis. My sacred companion refuses to budge."

Varloo tried to remember her cat lessons. She was pretty good at reading paw prints and could sometimes see meaning in the flick of a tail. But her cat tutor had told her nothing, at least nothing she remembered, about the meaning of a sacred cat that will not come when 'tis called.

"Methinks it signifies," Varloo told Osi, "that you are a stubborn cat."

Waiting for Osi to follow, Varloo dug around in her rucksack, searching for something to eat. She was supposed to conserve her food; Mother had written her a menu that dictated exactly what to eat when. The first meal was not to be until after a sleep, but she was hungry now. Longingly she thought of those mushroom cakes. There was nothing as delicious as that in her rucksack. Varloo unwrapped a food packet and took a tentative bite of the wafer inside. Oh, horrors! Turnip! She took another bite to be sure it was as bad as all that. Aye, it was.

But perhaps it would work as cat bait. "Come

hither, Osi-Osi. Varloo has a surprise for you," she said, tapping the odious wafer against the ground. The cat took a tentative step forward, sniffed, then turned up her nose too. But Varloo had hold of her by then and slipped the lead around her neck. "Now you must come with me," she said.

Down the steep hillside Varloo walked, tugging a reluctant Osi behind. The walking was difficult. Varloo's gown was awkward for hiking. Her mother's hat slipped over her face with every jolting step, and she stopped often to adjust it. Her shoulders ached with the weight of the necklace and the rucksack.

Varloo's training had included bodily fitness, but she had found many ways to shirk the most difficult exercises. When her tutor sent her to traverse the passageways of Hek, she took a shortcut and holed up in her favorite napping spot, behind the mill, where the *whump-whump-whump* of stones pounding wood into pulp lulled her to sleep.

As Varloo neared what she hoped was Stick Creek, she encountered a new obstacle, the squat vegetation growing on its banks. She had seen plants before—in the greenhouses and near the vents—but never anything so wild and profuse. Feeling daring, she pulled a leaf from one. Plants were so precious in Hek that only the farmers and harvesters were allowed to touch them.

Osi tried to nose her way underneath the bushes, but Varloo was too large to get through. Pulling the unhappy cat by its lead, she walked one way, then the other until she found an opening where someone had broken a narrow path. She turned sideways and edged down to the creek. Leaves scratched her face, and twigs tried to tug the hat from her head. At last she emerged and could see the water. It was nearly as wide as the River that flowed through the Park—several yards across, and it moved quickly.

Varloo's feet began to sink into the mud, and when she tried to extricate them by stepping onto a water-slick rock, she slid. She would have toppled splash into the creek, but Osi was straining toward the bank, and the cat's weight at the end of the lead pulled her back.

What to do? She did not know how to swim. Nor did Osi. If ever there was a time to consult her sacred companion, this appeared to be it.

"Osi-Osi-Osi," Varloo cooed. "Let me see you."

The Hekians believed cats to be sacred because their ancient stories told them this was true. Unfortunately the stories were maddeningly vague.

And, Varloo thought, there were certainly times when Osi did not behave even a trifling bit sacred.

Still, it did not hurt to try. So Varloo picked up her companion and studied the black depths of her fiery gold eyes. No bridge appeared there, no compass pointing the way, not even symbols for Varloo to decipher. She tried stroking the cat in hopes she would purr something intelligible, but Osi remained silent.

"Methinks you are no help," Varloo said. But as soon as the cat was set down, she pulled on her lead. Mayhap I should follow, Varloo thought. And soon enough, around a bend in the creek they came to a dead tree that spanned it like a bridge.

Even though Osi had led the way, she struggled when Varloo hoisted her up on the dead tree. The bark was damp against the cat's paws, and she lifted each one in turn, shook it with distaste, and set it back down in the wet.

"You will do better on your own now." Varloo unhooked the lead, then, with one hand on her hat, pulled herself up behind Osi. As she stood, her gown caught on a broken branch and tore, but she was too busy keeping her balance to care. The tree trunk was broad, but the bark was bumpy and slippery, and there were limbs to step over or around.

Varloo focused her eyes on the far bank, stood as tall as her small, round body allowed, and repeated to herself, "I am the first daughter of the first daughter." Heart pounding, she took one step, then another out over the water. The unhappy cat hesitated until Varloo was past, then followed.

A little more than halfway across, Varloo's foot caught in a knothole. She managed to stay upright by grabbing a branch, but as she teetered, the hat dropped into the creek and spun away downstream. Varloo had no time to mourn it. Osi didn't like that jiggling tree and wanted to leave it the fastest way possible. She took a great leap toward the bank but came up short and, before Varloo knew what was happening, there was a splash. Varloo watched in horror as her sacred companion floated downstream behind her mother's hat.

"O my Drake!" Varloo swore, and, forgetting her precarious position, ran the last few steps, then jumped to shore. With her eyes fixed on Osi's pathetic drenched head, Varloo slid and slipped along the creek side, breathing hard and trying to keep up.

"Osi!" she cried, tears splashing her cheeks. "I shall save you! Do not sink! Please, Osi—I need you!" But the water was carrying Osi faster even as

Varloo's footing grew more treacherous. Not looking where she was going, the girl almost ran headlong into a tree. She sidestepped at the last second but failed to see a rock jutting out of the shallow water and tumbled over it. Her head hit the rocky shore so hard her shaded spectacles bounced off.

Just before the blackness, she saw again the gold-bordered flap to her dwelling place in Hek—her home, where her mother waited for her.

Chapter Five

DOUGIE MINNERS WAS NOT dressed for church. He had on cutoffs and a torn T-shirt, old sneakers, and his beloved Oakland Raiders ball cap. His backpack was slung over his shoulder. Inside it were provisions: bubble gum stolen from his little brother Judah's not-so-secret stash, a bottle of water, and three big handfuls of Chips Ahoy! cookies.

Dougie had not fallen asleep till after midnight, but to avoid church he was willing to get up early. His parents had yet to come downstairs when he left his note on the kitchen table.

Dear Mom and Dad,
I am going out to the woods. I am sure you will agree that this is as good for my soul as church. I will try to bring back something for us to study.

> *Your favorite son,*
> *Dougie*

Dougie slipped out the back door and dashed silently across the yard. Once he was beyond the tree house, he whooped the Raiders' slogan—"Pride and poise!"—and took off running along the trail into the woods. His destination was the creek at the bottom of Spook Hill, where he planned to make an unscientific study of frogs, crawdads, and tadpoles.

In the Minners family Mom was considered the brains, Dad the practical one, Judah—age ten—the athlete, and Dougie . . . well, they hadn't figured that out yet. He was eleven years old and tall for his age. He liked science fiction and being outdoors. Every semester since second grade his teachers had put a "Code 9" on the comment section of his report card. Mom would tear open the envelope and shake her head as she read aloud: "Not working up to potential."

"Maybe I don't have that much potential," Dougie said once. Mom didn't think this was funny.

It was a couple of miles to the creek. Dougie ran through a stand of bull pine trees and oaks behind his subdivision, then slowed to a walk and climbed a hill colored with lupine and poppies. The morning was still cool but sunny and bright. The new grass smelled good. At the top of the hill was an overlook, and Dougie paused to eat a handful of broken cookies. Below him was a line of deep green that marked the course of the creek; ahead of him was Spook Hill—boulders, green spring grass, and a big old oak tree about halfway up; in the distance were the mountains capped with snow. When he turned around, he could see the neighborhood where his parents by now had spotted the empty cookie wrapper and shut the back door. Beyond that was the town of Oak Hollow, where they would be going to church with his little brother and without Dougie.

Another kid might have worried he'd get in trouble for skipping church. But Dougie was pretty sure his parents would forgive him. It would be good if he brought something back—a frog maybe, or a little snake. Then Dougie's dad would get a book off the shelf, and they'd look it up and try to identify it.

Dougie's parents were both what Suzy Shaeffer down the street called tree huggers, a phrase Suzy no doubt had learned from her father. What it meant was that they supported environmental causes like keeping dams from being built and protecting wild animals. In fact Dougie's mom was a lawyer and sometimes did environmental work for free. Suzy Shaeffer's dad was a lawyer too. But Dougie was sure he never did anything for free.

Dougie took his time descending the hill. The day was warm when at last he reached the bottom, and the coolness of the shade, mud, and water felt wonderful. He took off his shoes and splashed around the rocks, not caring if he scared away the creatures he had come to see. They would be back. He didn't mind waiting. He still had a piece of bubble gum and plenty of cookie crumbs in his backpack.

A bit upstream from the trail a dead tree had fallen across the creek. Still barefoot, Dougie climbed up on it and walked halfway across, gripping the rough bark with his toes. In the middle he pounded his fists on his chest and sang, "I am SuperDougie! King of the creek!" His voice was surprisingly tuneful. "I am hero of the hillsides! Lord of . . . uh . . . the crawdads!"

He bowed as if he were responding to applause, but the only real sounds were the music of flowing water, the *tap-tap-tap* of a woodpecker, the screech of a blue jay. So he dropped his hands to his side and shrugged. He wondered if he'd ever be anybody's hero. Heck, he wondered if he'd ever even "work up to potential."

He was splashing in the shallows a few minutes later when he thought he heard a sound that wasn't woodpecker, or water, or jay. Something like an animal's cry. A cat maybe? Whatever it was, it wasn't happy. Curious, Dougie laced on his sneakers to investigate.

He had gone about fifty yards, and the sound was becoming clearer, more like a whimper, when the fat trunk of a pine tree growing at the edge of the water blocked his path. Dougie waded into the creek to get around it, just avoiding a sharp rock in the water. He tried to get back to shore and almost stepped right on . . . her?

"Holy guacamole!" Dougie murmured. Here, in the shade of the tree, was the source of the sound—a pale, plump girl sort of thing that lay curled up on the rocks. Whatever it was had long light hair and paper-white skin. It wore a torn and muddy dress and a heavy gold necklace. There was a big backpack strapped to its shoulders. A pair of sunglasses lay, broken in two, on the ground a few feet away. One lens was shattered.

Dougie thought the girl thing was human—a kid—but he couldn't be sure. He only knew it was the weirdest sight he had laid eyes on in all his eleven years of life.

Chapter Six

As Judah Minners approached it on his bike, the lump of soggy gray fur on the shoulder of the highway looked like roadkill. But something about the way it lay there made him curious. Could it be alive? Did it need help?

Judah swung off his bike, thinking that it must have been a little like this to approach a dead animal in a trap. A mink? A fox? Judah's hero was Kit Carson, the legendary frontiersman and scout. Carson, he knew, had started out as a fur trapper.

But this animal wasn't a mink or a fox. And it wasn't dead either. The gray fur rose and fell as the creature breathed. A step later Judah recognized the pointed ears and long tail of a cat.

"Poor guy," said Judah. He wished he had a pair of gloves. The cat obviously was injured, and it wouldn't like being moved. He didn't want to be scratched or bitten, but he couldn't leave it to die either.

Judah knelt and put out his hand tentatively.

The cat opened its eyes and made a rumbling sound, a purr or a growl—Judah couldn't tell. He tried stroking the damp gray head and got no resistance, so he ran his hand down the back. The cat was well fed, he could see that. But there was no collar. Judah looked around. Down the embankment he could see Stick Creek as it flowed into a culvert beneath the roadway. Had someone tried to drown this poor cat?

Judah had been on his way to the minimart to get bubble gum and a bag of Skittles, his usual reward for putting up with church, but now he wondered if he had enough money for cat food instead. There was just one problem. His mother was allergic to cats. Could he keep this one in his room? She'd never go for it, and if he tried to hide it, she'd start sneezing.

Then he thought of something. The Minners family lived in an old house smack in the middle of a new subdivision. The land originally had been a cattle ranch, and theirs had been the ranch house. A ranch house with something new houses didn't have—a cellar.

It might work, Judah thought. Nobody ever went down there. Mom said the dust bothered her allergies. Dad said even seeing the place made him feel guilty because he should have cleaned it out long ago. Judah didn't mind dust or guilt. Eventually the cat might be discovered, but by then at least it would be healthy again.

Judah started planning. He could leave the bike here, carry the cat home, hide it in the cellar, come back, get his bike, and get cat food with the gum and Skittles money. Luckily his parents had gone out to lunch after church and wouldn't be back till later. And Dougie was . . . well, who knew? But Dougie didn't really matter. Even if he's home, Judah thought, he won't pay any attention to me.

Chapter Seven

With our ancestors
Borne on ships
Came the cats across the water.
Sacred are they, says the Story,
Devourers of pests. Wide-eyed. Wise.
Fed on fish, in Hek they flourish
Seeing far into the darkness.
One of them companion Osi,
Offspring of the sacred line,
Till the waters of the Surface
Bore her far away from me.
She was stubborn. She was lazy.
She was fat. And she complain'd.
Still I miss her and grieve for her
Solitary, far from home.

From the *Song of Varloo*, Sleep One

VARLOO'S HEAD ACHED. Her damp gown felt cold and clammy against her skin. She feared to open her eyes because the sky's brightness hurt terribly. And she missed Osi, her sacred companion, who was lost and probably drowned.

Varloo did not know exactly how she had gotten

to this place, but she did remember that she had help. Someone—a boy?—had half led, half dragged her for a distance that seemed endless. Her shaded spectacles had broken when she fell. Apparently the boy had recognized her distress because he put some queer kind of hat on her head. Even with it, she had not dared to open her eyes. That unnatural blue sky, the bright orb, how cruelly did they punish her.

Traveling blindly with the boy, she was aware only of the changing surface beneath her feet—broken, hard, rough, soft—and of the succession of strange smells. Finally her helper had hauled and pushed her up a ladder, then flopped her down here, taken the hat from her head, and said, "Be right back. Don't move." Later he had brought her a cushion, a blanket, a glass of water, and a handful of dry, sweet food. It was delicious—infinitely better than turnip wafers—and it made her hungrier.

The helper was an Extro, of course. Who else? And all Hekians knew the Extros as their enemies. It was part of a child's earliest teaching. The Extros in the land across the water had tried to destroy the Hekians once. That was why the Hekians had fled and eventually made their way underground.

It was why the Hekians sent a Spy to the Surface every fifty years—to see if anything the Extros did posed a threat to the civilization below. If the Extros ever were to learn about Hek, they would seek to destroy it. Varloo knew this as well as she knew that bats slept upside down.

But indeed it was not the Extro helper himself who worried Varloo most. She might be weakened by her ordeal, but still she was more clever than any Extro boy. She would never tell him about Hek or her Mission. What worried her most was what would happen to her when she returned home. Dazed and defenseless on the bank of the creek, Varloo had consorted herself with an Extro. She had violated the one Tenet that bound the Spy.

What would happen to her? She imagined there would be a trial before the Druids and then . . . what? Varloo had no idea. Not since Drasil had a Hekian committed so terrible an offense as Varloo had now. But Drasil had been a hero and so spared punishment. Long ago, though, in the early days of Hek, hadn't the Druids thrown wrongdoers into a bottomless Black Chasm that lay at the end of a hidden tunnel? There was a song about this. Some people said the song was true.

Varloo was worried about what would happen

to her. And she was angry that her Mission had gone so wrong so fast. But Varloo also was thinking about something else.

Cookies.

She was hoping that the boy, the helper, would return soon and that he would bring more of that delicious sweet food. Cookies he called them. They were better than mushroom cakes.

Varloo heard footsteps below her. Through her eyelashes she peeked out at a brown wall, apparently made from wood. When she opened her eyes a little wider, she saw she was in a shelter that seemed to be part of a tree not unlike the sacred oak. What an odd place for a shelter, she thought.

The structure shook, and a second later the helper's head, under its black and silver hat, appeared at the opening in the wall.

"Hey, you're sitting up," he said. "Do you feel better? Can you talk yet? I brought more cookies."

"Cookies." Varloo said the unfamiliar word eagerly. "May I have another, please?"

"I brought a whole box. I hope Mom doesn't miss 'em. Hey, you speak English." He handed her the package.

"Did you expect that I should speak French?" she asked through a mouthful. The helper laughed, and Varloo opened her eyes wide. From the Story she knew that Extros laughed. But to actually see it and hear it was frightening.

"It's a funny kind of English, though," the helper was saying. "Not like American. Where are you from anyway? Outer space, right?" Varloo was speechless, still trying to get over her surprise at the helper's laughter. "Yoo-hoo? Earth to Alien?" He looked at her quizzically. "Are you okay? I don't know what you should speak. I just thought in outer space they talked in clicks or beeps or something. But then you're not green or a lizard either, so I guess I was wrong about a lot of things."

Varloo swallowed hard. It made her nervous to see all those teeth in the Extro's smile. In Hek the only people who smiled were babies. But she did not want him to know she was frightened by his bizarre behavior. So she said weakly, "Where is outer space?"

"You know, up in the sky. Isn't that where you're from? I figured a flying saucer left you. Like E.T."

Varloo's aching head was muddled. So much she did not understand. Flying saucer? E.T.? But she could not admit her ignorance to an Extro.

"Aye," she said slowly. "'Tis exactly as you say. My home is in the sky. A flying plate has brought me to this place. E.T. is my, uh . . . sister."

The helper had a queer look on his face. Had she said something wrong?

"You're faking," he said at last. "But if it's a costume, it's really good." He shook his head. "Anyway, I should tell you my name, huh? If you're gonna stay in my tree house. I'm Dougie—Dougie Minners. Douglas Bartholomew Minners, but nobody ever uses the Bartholomew. Hardly anybody even knows about the Bartholomew, and I don't know why I told you. You can laugh if you want. Anybody would."

"You need not worry yourself," Varloo said. "We never laugh."

"Never?" The helper looked stunned. "There's like a law against it where you come from?"

"A Tenet, you mean? 'Tis not necessary. To laugh would be unthinkable."

The helper shook his head. "But why? I don't get it."

"Since the time of Uther it has been forbidden," Varloo explained, but the boy's face showed that he still did not understand. "The ordeal of the Ancestors across the water began when the others did laugh at them for their different beliefs, for their superior wisdom and knowledge. In the end the

35

Ancestors were forced to flee, to come here to Nova Albion. Now do you see?"

The boy pushed up the brim on his black and silver cap. "Whatever you say."

Varloo had not meant to mention the Ancestors across the water. But she wanted this Extro to understand her. She tried again. "What do you feel when you are laughed at?"

"I feel bad," Dougie admitted. "But let me ask something else: Do you cry?"

"Indeed we cry," Varloo said. "Should we not have feelings?"

"Well, that doesn't seem fair then. I mean, laughing is like the flip side of crying. If you do one without the other . . . it can't be good for you. You get unbalanced."

Varloo had never heard anything more absurd. But it was her own fault. She had tried to explain civilized behavior to an Extro. Better simply to see what other food he had brought her.

"Douglas Bartholomew Minners," Varloo repeated, "my name is Varloo."

"Varloo. Cool. Varloo what?"

"Is Varloo not sufficient?"

"Well, you know, like I've got three names and . . ." Varloo looked at him. "Yeah . . . well, anyway, here—I brought you a Tylenol for your headache and a jug of Kool-Aid, plus I found some potato chips. Do you like potato chips?"

"Aye," Varloo said. Potatoes she knew. They tasted fine. Chips? She would try them.

The helper was still talking. "You've got to stay here in the tree house, okay? At least till you feel better and I figure out what to do. If Judah saw you, I don't know what'd happen. He'd probably call 9–1–1. You know what that is?"

"Aye," said Varloo.

The helper grinned and shook his head. "You're faking."

Chapter Eight

SUZY SHAEFFER HOPPED OFF her bike in front of Dougie's house and bumped the kickstand with her heel. It wouldn't budge. She bumped it harder, but still it stayed put. Rusted.

"Stupid bike," Suzy grumbled, and she pushed it across the driveway so she could lean it against the side of the garage, out of sight. Then she pulled a book from the basket that was attached to the handlebars.

Suzy Shaeffer figured her bike was the most embarrassing in the world. It was a pink Barbie bike she had gotten when she was little, hopeless for a kid her age, besides which it had gotten old and rusty. Her dad had raised the seat till the bolt was on its absolutely last hole. It had a dirty white basket and faded purple tassels. It was hideous.

Suzy had asked for two things this year at Christmas. A guitar. And a mountain bike. She didn't get either one. Suzy's mom said Suzy didn't have time to practice guitar because she was too busy with horseback riding.

Suzy's dad said Suzy could have a new bike only when (1) she grew enough so she needed it, (2) people bought a whole bunch of the lots he was planning to sell on the hillside across the creek, and (3) she cleaned up the rust and gunk on the old one so they could sell it at a yard sale.

Her dad's habit of talking in one, two, three order came from being a lawyer. It was a real pain to argue with him because he always sounded organized, even if what he said didn't make that much sense. Anyway, Suzy's dad was still a lawyer, but now he was also planning—in his words—"to make some real money" buying big hunks of land, then selling pieces of it as lots for houses.

Suzy wasn't going to say anything about those lots to Dougie. He and his family were all into environmental stuff. She didn't think they would approve.

Suzy climbed the three front steps and knocked on the Minnerses' front door. Dougie's dad answered.

"Hey, nice to see you, Suzy," Leo Minners said. "We've missed you around here. You looking for Doug?"

"Yes, sir. I brought his *War of the Worlds* back."

She held the paperback up for Dougie's dad to see.

"H. G. Wells at his finest," said Mr. Minners. "How did you like it?"

"Well . . . actually, I didn't read it. The idea was dumb. I mean, Martians? Not likely, sir. Do you know what daytime temperatures are on Mars?"

"Hot?" Mr. Minners asked.

"Cold!" said Suzy. "Like minus one hundred and fifty degrees, and that's at the equator. I'm asking you, what kind of creatures could live in that weather?"

Dougie's dad shook his head. "No telling. But maybe stark realism wasn't exactly the point?"

Suzy smiled. "Mr. Minners, you can't have truth without facts."

Leo Minners grinned. "Too deep for me. I work in a bank. But I know Doug will be glad to get his book—and to see you. He ditched church to go out in the woods, and now I think he's avoiding me in case he's in trouble. He'll probably show up for dinner, though. You hungry?"

"No, thank you," said Suzy. "We're having McDonald's."

"Fine idea," said Mr. Minners, "ketchup being a vegetable and all. Come on through if you want to find Doug. Try the tree house maybe."

Suzy trotted through the hallway and the kitchen and out the back door. It had been a long time since she had visited Dougie. It felt sort of weird. If she told herself the truth, she knew returning this crummy old book was just an excuse. She missed him and the things they used to do together. At the same time she had a lot of new friends from the stable where she took riding lessons—girlfriends—and she liked hanging with them and talking about horses and hair and who kissed who at the movies.

Dougie didn't care about stuff like that. In some ways he was pretty immature.

The tree house was invisible from the back porch. But Suzy could see the top branches of the oak that held it. "Dougie!" she hollered. "Where are you anyway? Dougie-e-e-e-e-e!"

The first faint stars had appeared in the sky. Mom would be wanting her back so they could go into town and get dinner. Probably she should leave the book in the kitchen and ride her bike home. I'll just run out to the tree house first and check, she thought.

She took off across the backyard, enjoying the free feeling of running fast. She was almost to the forsythia bushes that bordered the lawn when she saw dark shapes flittering above her head.

Weird time for all these birds, she thought. Then she realized that they weren't birds at all. They were bats.

And Suzy just hated bats.

"Oh, yuck!" She closed her eyes, put the book over her head, and stood very still. Please go away, she thought. Please don't get in my hair!

From somewhere she heard stomping and rustling and then the familiar voice. "Suzy? Jeez, you scared us—I mean me, uh, half to death! What are you doing out here? And why do you have a book on your head?"

"Bats." Suzy choked the word out.

"Oh, for golly jeez," Dougie said. "Just because one got in your house that time. Haven't I told you bats are the good guys? They eat like a thousand times their weight in mosquitoes every night! Come on in the house, and I'll—"

Suzy opened one eye and looked up. The bats seemed to be gone. "They get tangled in hair," she said. "They do. Everybody knows that."

"They don't get tangled in hair! That's what Mom calls an old husbands' tale. Come on back in the house, and—"

"I brought your book." Suzy moved it off her head cautiously.

"Great," Dougie said. But he didn't even glance at it. Instead he looked over his shoulder and at the same time grabbed Suzy's hand, which Suzy yanked away. What did he think he was doing?

"You busy out here?" Suzy was curious. Dougie seemed weird.

"No. Not busy. Hunh-unh. Just hanging out. You know." Dougie tried again to steer her to the house.

"What's the matter with you?" she asked. "Have you got something back there in the tree?" She tried to get around him, but he stepped sideways and blocked her.

"Uh-oh, Suzy, look! They're coming this way!" Dougie pointed at the sky, but Suzy didn't look; she shut her eyes tight and covered her head.

"Where? I hate bats!"

"You're right," he said. "Nasty things! We better get you into the house quick—with your long hair and all. . . ."

Eyes closed, Suzy let him push her across the yard. She peeked only after she was back on the porch. "Where'd they go?"

"Away," Dougie answered. "But it was a close call. I think one was diving for your head!"

Dougie opened the door, and Suzy ducked into the Minnerses' kitchen. She was flustered by the marauding flocks of bats, but she was also confused. "I thought you said bats are good," she told Dougie.

"They are," he said.

"Then how come you called them nasty?"

A car horn interrupted before Dougie could answer. "That's Mom," Suzy said. "I guess I gotta go."

Dougie followed her out the front door. "Hi, Doug," Suzy's mom called from the car. "Nice to see you."

Suzy slammed the passenger door shut and waved. She was still confused. Had her ex–best friend tricked her? But why would he want her out of his backyard?

The ride to the Oak Hollow McDonald's was short. Only ten minutes later Mom was placing the order at the drive-through. That was when Suzy remembered. She had left her crummy old bike outside the Minnerses' garage.

Chapter Nine

How palatable are the Extros' foods,
The french fried potatoes,
The sauce from tomatoes,
The Oreo cookies with the sweet,
*   white paste.*
O various are the Extros' foods!
And hastily must I eat them.

From the *Song of Varloo*, Sleep One

WHEN THE GIRL EXTRO had called out, disturbing their conversation, the helper had almost fallen out of the tree house in his haste to intercept her. Varloo had heard voices, then silence. Now, apparently, the danger had passed, but the helper had not returned.

Varloo worried that this tree house, near as it was to the Extro shelter, might not be a safe refuge for the Spy. But her head hurt her, and moving did seem like so much trouble. For now she would stay here and hope the helper did continue to keep intruders away.

In the twilight Varloo found that she could leave her eyes open, provided she did not look upward. Still, she longed for the broken shaded spectacles. They would make her eyes so much more comfortable.

She picked up the bottle the helper had brought earlier. It contained white tablets. There were markings on the bottle, somewhat like the symbols on her map. Varloo remembered from her lessons that the Extros had something called letters, and they used them for communication. This further signifies the Extros' stupidity, Varloo thought. It must be that they do not have the intelligence to memorize their own Story, or the music to sing their own Songs.

Varloo twisted and twisted the cap, frustrated that it did not open. Finally she happened to press and twist the cap at once. *Pop*—the bottle opened, scattering tablets everywhere. Hoping it might be as delicious as cookies, she picked one up, put it into her mouth, and bit down.

Oh, horrid and bitter—worse than a turnip wafer! She spit it out. Perhaps Douglas Bartholomew Minners is wicked, trying to poison me, she thought. But that was not sensible. He would not have wasted those delicious, sweet cookies if he did mean for me to perish. Perhaps the white tablets were some variety of elixir, like the one her mother used when she was bilious? Still, I will not bite another, she thought.

She turned next to the flat crunchy disks in the little bag. Licking one, she recognized the flavor of potatoes but thought the taste better than any potato she had ever eaten. So deliciously salty and greasy! She gobbled down all that were in the bag, and this made her thirsty. She sampled the pink liquid and discovered it was nearly as tasty as cookies.

I wonder how it is that the Extros eat so well when they are so stupid, Varloo thought. 'Tis a shame they are our enemies.

By the time Varloo licked the potato crumbs out of the bag, ate half the cookies, and finished the sweet drink, the sky was completely dark, and she could open her eyes comfortably. She peered over the side of her shelter and saw she was about ten feet above the ground. There were smaller trees around her, and through them she could see the glow of lanterns inside the large shelter where the helper lived. A few bats flitted above her, and she eyed them carefully. Part of Geber's herd, she thought. They are so free, compared with me. They come and go from Hek to the Surface in a way that no Hekian may.

47

But I must not dwell on such matters, she said to herself. I have much work to do, and if I sink into loneliness, it will be too hard for me.

The air had grown cool again, and Varloo's damp gown chilled her. From her rucksack she took her second gown and changed into it. Then she hung the damp gown over the wall of the shelter to dry. Time to tidy up, she thought, and brushed the bottle the helper had given her, along with the scattered white tablets, through a gap in the wall. She folded and arranged her own blanket along with the one Dougie had brought and made herself cozy. She was about to begin composing a verse of her Song when she saw a beam of light dancing among the branches and heard the helper coming back.

"Do not shine that light at my face!" Varloo snapped, shutting her eyes. There was a click, and the light disappeared.

"Sorry," Dougie said. "Here. I brought you these. New sunglasses. They're an old pair of Mom's. She'll never miss 'em."

"Shaded spectacles!" Varloo reached for them eagerly.

"Yeah," said Dougie. "Shades."

Varloo placed them over her eyes and ears,

noticing that they were made of some queer, light material, much more comfortable than the ones she had broken in her fall. And they worked well. Now Varloo could open her eyes wide and study the helper for the first time.

He was tall but pathetically thin, she saw. His face was unattractively tan, the cheeks pinkish. His tiny eyes were the color of mud, and so was what little hair she could see beneath his black and silver hat.

Varloo felt a pang of sympathy. These Extros were not only stupid but ugly too.

"They look good," the helper said. "And you're welcome, by the way. I brought you this too. Leftovers. We had hamburgers and french fries, and Judah didn't finish his. He never eats anything but Count Chocula." The food he handed her on a plate had been nibbled and looked limp, but it was sure to be better than anything she had brought from Hek. "It's got ketchup on it, and pickles," Dougie said, "just like McDonald's. That's where Suzy was going for dinner. I have to tell you about Suzy. It was a close call. Do they have McDonald's where you live?"

"McDonald's," Varloo repeated. "Aye, indeed." The food reminded her a little of mushrooms. She particularly liked the sweet red sauce on it. The long, skinny things were good too—another form of potato. These Extros did certainly favor potatoes. She wondered if she should say anything about this observation in her Song.

"So like I said," Dougie went on, "Suzy. She was the one hollering in the yard before, who almost came out here and found you? We used to be best friends, but now she's all into horses and girl junk. She might've come all the way back here too. But the bats came and scared her—"

"Frightened by bats?" Varloo stopped chewing. "Preposterous!"

"Well, sure it is," Dougie said. "They don't scare me. Not that I'd want to be up close and personal with one. But like I was saying, I saved you for the second time because I told her the bats were diving at her head, and then she ran into the house."

"Bats have no interest in heads," Varloo said.

"Well, I know that," said Dougie. "But she doesn't. And I'm not sure you're getting my point here. I rescued you again! For the second time in one day! So now I guess you're grateful, huh?"

Varloo did not reply but instead considered the helper. He did not understand anything, but how could he be expected to? She was the Spy of an ancient civilization. He was merely an Extro boy. She had not intended to tell him anything of her people, but mayhap she would need to. So long as she was in this shelter in this tree, she must needs rely on him. Mayhap he could even share his knowledge of the Extro world. This would help her with her spying.

She chewed a few more bites of the delicious food, thinking how much the red sauce did please her. Then she realized that the helper did stare, and now he shook his head. "Holy guacamole!" he said. "I never saw anybody so hungry!"

Chapter Ten

DOUGIE HAD TO WORK FAST. It was Monday morning, and the class got only half an hour in the library. He was supposed to be finding books for his report. Instead he punched J-O-K-E-S into the computer, then went over to the 793 section where all eight titles were supposed to be. He pulled out the first one and sat on the floor to copy riddles. He had two done when somebody trying to get by bumped his knee.

"Hey, watch where you're going!" Dougie was grumpy because he'd gone to bed so late. He and Varloo had talked till he said he had to go in or his parents would come looking. Now he looked up and saw the person who had bumped him was Suzy Shaeffer. "Oh, hi," he said. "Thanks for bringing my book back yesterday."

"No problem." She looked down at the joke books. "I thought you were writing about caves."

"This is something different," he said.

"If Mrs. Wilkerson sees you, you'll get in trouble."

Suzy drove Dougie nuts sometimes. "Thanks for your input," he said.

She frowned and walked off toward the books about horses.

Dougie copied two lightbulb jokes from the book on the floor. Then he went back to the computer and typed in C-A-V-E. About twenty titles popped up, too many for Dougie to sort through before the bell rang.

"Try 'Calaveras County caves.'" Dougie was so startled he jumped. It was Mrs. Wilkerson, looking over his shoulder. Had Suzy really snitched? he wondered. But he did as the teacher suggested. This time there was one book and two magazine articles. "That's more reasonable, isn't it?" she asked.

"Thanks," Dougie said.

"Don't mention it. Say . . . Doug?"

"Huh? I mean, yes?"

"I'd like to see you do an extra-good job on this paper," Mrs. Wilkerson said. "Caves are a fascinating subject, and we're fortunate to have so many right here. Have you visited any of them?"

"Yeah, sure, lots of times," Dougie said, "with my mom."

"That's fine," she said. "You might want to add

some postcards or photographs to your report. Or . . . didn't I see something in the newspaper about caves this morning? About the lost caves under Spook Hill?" Dougie shrugged. He read the newspaper only when the Raiders were playing. "Take a look," Mrs. Wilkerson said. "I don't have to remind you—you could use the extra credit."

Dougie nodded. When he had brought Varloo back to the tree house yesterday, he was half tempted to tell his dad about her so they could look her up in some book, the way they did with toads and snakes. Now Dougie wondered how much extra credit he'd get if he brought a real live cave dweller to school to go with his report.

It had taken almost the whole box of Oreos, but finally last night she had stopped faking and told him the truth, or at least he thought it was the truth. She didn't come from space at all, but from a whole civilization called Hek that lived in a secret limestone cavern. From what she said, he thought it must be under Spook Hill. She was a "spy" from the civilization, sent to what she called "the surface" to make sure nothing up here threatened Hek.

"You mean they send kids?" Dougie had asked. "Girls? For such an important job?"

"Every fifty years," she said. "My grandmother

was the last. 'Tis our tradition to send the first daughter of the first daughter. The wise Ancestors believed both that a girl would provoke less hostility should she be discovered and that a girl would be less inclined to hot temper." Then she told him that she had been well trained for spying and, besides, that she was not expected to find much to threaten Hek on her mission.

"During the last two missions—after the time of the hero Drasil—the Spies did find no sign of Extro habitation near to us," she said. Now she was surprised at the number of "shelters," as she called them, in Dougie's neighborhood.

Varloo's story about the two Spies before her made sense, Dougie realized. This Drasil Spy must have come during the Gold Rush, and since then the California foothills had quieted down. There had been a few ranches like the one his house had been part of; there had been logging camps in the mountains. But Oak Hollow had been almost a ghost town for one hundred years. That didn't change until the 1970s and 1980s, when people like his parents and the Shaeffers started moving to "the country" from California's big cities. Now Calaveras County was one of the fastest-growing parts of the state.

Another kid might not have believed Varloo's story, Dougie thought. He wasn't sure why he did. Maybe his mom was right, and he read too much science fiction. But Dougie thought Varloo's story made a weird kind of sense. If there was going to be some underground civilization, Spook Hill was a good place for it. Dougie had heard that the name came from some old story about ghosts or monsters that lived there. Nobody ever went to Spook Hill, partly because of the stories but also because it was private property.

Anyway, Dougie had no better explanation for a short, pale-faced, chubby blond girl in a long robe who talked funny. Since Varloo herself was so strange, it was logical that her explanation would be strange too.

She had also told him something else: "'Tis imperative that you do keep my secret. For if the Extros were to discover us, we would be destroyed."

"Just like the Indians." Dougie had studied California history in school last year, so he knew how most of the Indians had died of disease, or else starved, or else been murdered, after the pioneers came. The Indian civilization had been overwhelmed by another one that was so much bigger. He could see how the same thing would happen to Varloo's.

Now Dougie glanced up from the library floor and saw Suzy taking notes on her horse book. He bet Suzy wouldn't have believed Varloo. Suzy had no imagination at all. Plus she was scared of measly little bats, for gosh sake. If she had found Varloo, she would've first been terrified and then snitched and been responsible for destroying an entire civilization.

Dougie had tried to tell Varloo she was lucky he had been the one to find her and rescue her. Twice. I mean, Dougie said, I'm practically a hero doing this, right? But maybe not. Varloo didn't even say thank you.

Then there was this business of not smiling or laughing. It was annoying. Nothing made her smile, not even when he tried to tickle her feet; that just made her mad. So now Dougie was determined to make her laugh, if he had to copy down every joke in the library to do it. Laughing would be good for her.

Chapter Eleven

AFTER SCHOOL THAT DAY Dougie threw his library books on the kitchen table and yelled hello to his mom.

"Hello, honey!" she called back from her office upstairs. Then he heard her sneeze, and there was the snuffly sound of a person blowing her nose. Poor Mom, he thought. She's working so hard she's caught a cold.

The bowl on the kitchen table was full of apples, which meant she had gone to the store. Dougie ignored the apples, opened a drawer under the counter, stepped up on it, and reached to the highest cupboard shelf, where the new box of cookies would be.

Oh, good—Oreos. He put handfuls in each pocket for Varloo, then stuffed a couple in his mouth and got a glass of milk.

"Where's the scuzzface?" he hollered up. Mom must have a deadline coming up, he thought. Otherwise she would have come downstairs to ask how school was.

"If you mean your only brother, he's at Little League practice," she called back. "I have to pick him up at five."

Plenty of time to steal some bubble gum, Dougie thought. Judah could not possibly be dumber about his stash, in Dougie's opinion. First, he kept it in the most obvious hiding place in the world, his underwear drawer. Second, he never noticed any was missing.

Dougie sat down at the kitchen table to eat his snack. The newspaper was still on the chair where his dad had left it that morning, so he picked it up and turned the pages, looking for the story Mrs. Wilkerson had mentioned. There it was, page A-3:

DEVELOPER EYES SPOOK HILL

Old-timers speak of ghosts;

Shaeffer sees 1,000 homesites

Oak Hollow—Lawyer-turned-developer LeRoy Shaeffer will go before the planning commission Wednesday seeking permits to build Collina Fantastica, a gated community of some 1,000 homes on a tract of land that includes the notorious Spook Hill.

LeRoy Shaeffer? That's Suzy's dad, Dougie thought. I didn't know he was a developer now. Dougie kept reading.

* * *

Shaeffer says scary tales of missing miners, ghostly sightings, and even a race of man-eating trolls living in caves don't bother him, and they won't bother home buyers.

"Heck, those old stories will probably be good for business," Shaeffer said at a press conference to announce his purchase of the land for the project. "Romance of the Old West and all that."

Environmentalists are poised to fight the project, citing two objections. One is Stick Creek, which flows through the ravine at the base of the hill.

"It's a fragile riparian habitat that deserves protection," said Doria Capehart of the Foothill Defense Fund (FDF).

The second objection relates to the "lost caves" that local lore places beneath Spook Hill itself. Capehart pointed out that if caves exist, they may be home to a number of ecologically significant creatures.

"Naturalists suspect a migrant maternity colony of Mexican free-tailed bats roosts somewhere near Oak Hollow," Capehart explained. "And Spook Hill is a likely location. It's so seldom visited that the bats could come and go with no one the wiser."

Pressed to say whether she believes the bats are really there, Capehart shrugged. "No one has ever been willing to devote the resources to finding out," she said. "And when I say 'resources,' what I mean is money."

Besides bats, other rare creatures, including salamanders, insects, and fish, may live in the caves, Capehart said.

And what about trolls?

"If they're there, they deserve protection too," Capehart said.

In spite of environmentalists' vow to fight, developer Shaeffer said he is confident county planners will give him the go-ahead when they meet Wednesday night.

"The earthmovers are rarin' to go," said Shaeffer. "By this time next year we'll be framing houses on Spook Hill."

Dougie's eyes got big. He had asked Varloo lots of questions last night but never if she was a man-eating troll. Were the Hekians not human at all? Were they trolls? Did they eat humans? Did *Varloo* eat humans? Dougie shivered as he thought of the girl who was probably, at this moment, curled up asleep in his tree house. She had told him about her training. How did you train a Spy, anyway? Like 007 kind of training?

Maybe she was dangerous. Maybe protecting a being from another world wasn't such a hot idea. Hek's survival wasn't really his problem, was it? Maybe it would be a whole lot safer if he did tell somebody about her.

Chapter Twelve

Gathered round the flick'ring boxes,
Dumbly watch, always watch,
Parents, children, elders watch
Pretty lives of shadow Extras,
Music, dancing, feats of magic.
Toothy laughter—ever fright'ning.
Spectacle is all.

From the *Song of Varloo*, Sleep Two

SOMETHING WAS DIFFERENT about the helper. Varloo discerned this at once from the noisy way he ascended into her tree house.

"I'm not giving you any Oreos tonight." The helper's frown matched that of the one-eyed man pictured on his black and silver hat.

Varloo was cautious. "As you wish."

"I might not give you any dinner either."

This would be a sore disappointment. Varloo had the turnip wafers and other foods from home, but all the sleeping day she had dreamed of foods described by the helper last night—pizza and egg rolls and goldfish crackers.

Varloo controlled herself and answered again,

"As you wish. You may leave me to my composing then."

Her outward calm seemed to confuse him. "I didn't say for sure I wouldn't give you anything."

"Then do say it now, I pray. Do I dine? Or not?"

"You have to answer some questions first," he said.

"More questions!"

"How do I know you're telling the truth?"

Varloo fixed him with her gaze. "I will be truthful if I am sufficiently fed."

Now the helper looked flustered. But then he sighed and opened the bag he was carrying. Out came a plate covered with paper clear as glass. Through it she could see a messy red and white mass.

"It's lasagna," he said. "You've never had that, right?"

Varloo no longer lied about trifles. Indeed she suspected she may have said more to this Extro than ever she had intended. "No," she told him now. "It has the red sauce, though. The red sauce I like." The helper handed Varloo a plate and a fork. She unwrapped the clear paper and took a bite. The food was pleasantly mushy. There were even mushrooms in it, which made her think of home.

Dougie explained that this red sauce was different from the ketchup from last night, but it tasted the same to Varloo.

"So what I want to know is this," Dougie said. "Are you a man-eating troll?"

Varloo had not been tempted to laugh since she saw Geber slip on a pile of guano when she was three years old. But now she was almost overcome. She clamped her lips shut to keep from spitting lasagna. One corner of her mouth curled dangerously.

So the Extros have stories just as we do, she thought. And it seems they still tell of Drasil's spectacle.

Partly to control her rebellious face, she sang a verse of Drasil's Song:

> *"Loudly clanging,*
> *Ever banging,*
> *Entrails gushing blood,*
> *Howl and howling,*
> *Scowl and yowling,*
> *Fast the Extros fled."*

Drasil had been a better hero than poet, Varloo reflected.

"Hey, what's that?" Dougie asked her. "What're you singing about? I didn't know you could sing."

"We all do sing," said Varloo. "While we work. On sacred days. And because it pleases us."

Dougie smiled. "Singing," he said. "That's really cool. But answer my question. Are you trolls or what?"

Best to tell the truth, Varloo decided. What would the helper do if he thought she really might eat him? "I am not a troll," she said decisively. "Do you have more questions?"

"Yeah," Dougie said. "I'm just getting started. If that's what you're not, what are you?"

"I am a human being! Just as you are. 'Tis the life underground that does make our appearance so pleasing."

The helper's eyes widened. "You think you're better-looking than us?"

"'Tis plain," said Varloo. "But there is hope for you Extros, methinks. Perhaps if you did eat more? There is an abundance of palatable food here on the Surface." Varloo scraped the utensil called fork across her plate and licked it.

Dougie shook his head. "How come you live underground in the first place?"

Varloo could not help but mimic his queer way

of speaking: "'How come' you live on the Surface?"

"I asked you first," he said.

Varloo could see he was no longer angry. Perhaps he even had brought some Oreos, tucked into his pockets. "Did I not tell you of the ordeal of the Ancestors across the water? After Uther was taken from us, we did flee that land in fear of our lives." She hoped that would satisfy him, but it did not.

"Who in the world is Uther?"

Varloo sighed. Would she never get her Oreos? "Uther was the great Druid and alchemist who inspired the Ancestors and foretold our coming to this place, Nova Albion, which you do call California. It was Uther who studied the Emerald Tablet of the alchemists and the ancient lore of the pagans. It was Uther who unified those beliefs, Uther who taught his followers the lost secrets of alchemy."

"Alchemy?" Dougie asked. "You mean like Merlin, right? Turning lead into gold?"

Varloo shook her head. "'Tis impossible to transform a base metal into gold, helper. Even you Extros know that."

"Then I don't understand what you're talking about," the helper said. "Besides, how can you live underground anyway? I don't know a lot about science, but I know plants need light, and so do animals. How can you grow anything in the dark?"

"'Tis not dark. We have harnessed the secrets of alchemical electricity, of magnetism, of the guano of the bats and of the flowing water. With them, we create light. And much more," Varloo said.

"It sounds crazy," said Dougie.

"Exactly," said Varloo. "To the Extros, 'tis crazy. And for that reason do we live apart."

Dougie was thoughtful for a minute. "So you're saying a long time ago, a long, long time ago, you guys lived up here like us?"

"Aye, helper. The Ancestors lived on the Surface, far across the water. But we have never eaten men, helper. In the name of the great Drake, I do swear it. And furthermore, I will not eat you. I do not know even the best way to cook you. And methinks you would not taste as good as this . . . *lasagna*."

Dougie laughed. Ordinarily his laughter made Varloo cringe, but tonight she felt relief. "Where did you get this idea," she asked, "that I am a man-eating troll? Do you sing this Song in your school?"

Dougie laughed again and told her about the newspaper article and Suzy Shaeffer's dad. As

Varloo listened to his story, she felt her chest tighten and her face flush. She even forgot about Oreos. "Bring to me this paper," she said, "at once. You must sing to me this Song you say is there."

Dougie snorted. "Would you stop ordering me around? I'm just as good as you, you know. Better, if you want my opinion. Anyway, I don't sing."

Varloo closed her eyes and tried to think clearly. She must not panic. She would make the helper understand. He would do as he had been told.

Chapter Thirteen

DOUGIE DIDN'T EXACTLY GET what was eating her, but Varloo sounded so upset that he ran back to the house, got the newspaper clipping off his desk, and put it in his pocket.

Coming through the kitchen again, he almost ran into Judah, who was fixing himself a bowl of cereal. "Should've eaten dinner, blockhead," Dougie said. He tried to knock the 49ers cap off his brother's head at the same time Judah went for Dougie's Raiders cap.

"Ni-i-i-i-iners!" Judah hollered, and punched the air.

"Pride and poise," Dougie replied.

Judah poured milk on his cereal. "What did you do with the leftover lasagna anyway, idiot breath?"

"Snooze y'lose, moron," Dougie answered.

"What are you doing in the backyard anyway, snotpot?" Judah took a bite. "Fattening up a squirrel?"

Dougie was so surprised he forgot to call his

brother a name. "What do you mean?"

"I mean, babybutt, last night and tonight half the kitchen disappeared after dinner; then you disappeared with it. You got a girlfriend you're feeding?" The thought was so hilarious that Judah almost choked on his Count Chocula.

"Ha-ha," Dougie said feebly.

"Kit Carson would've tracked you back there to see what it was you were hiding," Judah said.

"Yeah, well"—Dougie pushed the door open—"you're no Kit Carson."

The idea of Varloo as anybody's girlfriend was sick, but Judah's stupid guess was too close to the truth. Dougie looked over his shoulder as he ran across the yard, but nobody was following. The overgrown corner where the tree house was had always been his private territory. Judah called it the creepy zone and teased him about hanging out in poison oak with tarantulas and rattlesnakes.

Judah was too chicken to actually come back here—wasn't he?

Dougie climbed the ladder again.

"Give me the paper," Varloo said.

"Can't you even say please?"

"Please," she said. But it still sounded like an order. Feeling resentful, Dougie reached into his pocket and handed her the clipping. She studied it a minute—both upside down and right side up—then handed it back. "Sing it to me. Please."

"You mean you can't read?"

"Of course not," said Varloo. "Only my mother, the Ovate, can read. The lore of reading is passed down from one Ovate to the next so that we do not lose it. The rest of us have no need to read. We remember our Songs and remember our Story even as Uther did remember the Emerald Tablet."

Dougie shook his head. Ovate? Emerald Tablet? Anyway, these Hekian people must be pretty darn dumb if they can't even read, he thought. But there was never any point arguing with Varloo. "I can't sing," said Dougie. "I'll just say it, okay?" He started in on the story about LeRoy Shaeffer's plan for Spook Hill. Halfway through he looked up: "I'm not always gonna let you order me around."

Varloo said nothing; he went on reading.

"When is summer?" she asked after he was done.

Dougie resisted the urge to ask how come she didn't know anything at all. "Summer is when we get off school. It's the hottest time of year. June it starts—in about a month."

"What is bulldozer?"

71

"Um, hmm . . . well, it's a giant machine with like a shovel thing on it. To push dirt around."

Varloo turned paler even than usual, and for the first time Dougie thought he saw why. It was like what his mom and dad were always telling him: If you did something that affected one thing in nature, you affected everything else too. So if Mr. Shaeffer moved around a bunch of dirt, he'd also be moving around the plants and animals and bugs that lived in the dirt. And maybe even the caves underneath the dirt.

What if the bulldozers caused a cave-in? Or what if the noise scared the bats away? Varloo kept saying how her people needed bats because bat poop—she called it guano—made fertilizer for their farms and even, if he understood her right, medicine. Today she had said something about bat poop and electricity. It seemed hard to believe, but then the existence of Varloo herself was hard to believe too.

"Holy guacamole." Dougie felt stupid. "I didn't realize . . . I mean, I wouldn't want big heavy machines on the roof of my house either."

Varloo nodded. "As the Spy, I must stop this wicked Extro called LeRoy Shaeffer."

"Stop him? But you have to go back Thursday

night, don't you? You don't exactly have a lot of time."

Varloo looked thoughtful. "Neither did the hero have much time," she said.

Chapter Fourteen

O! The Extro children have hard lives.
All the bright, cruel day do they toil
     in the school.
Then falls the sun, how welcome
     the darkness!
But still the children may not rest,
For terrible is their homework.
How it does tax their poor brains,
And tiresome are the chores
With which their parents do
     oppress them—
The dishes to wash,
The bedrooms to clean,
The grass that must be mowed
     and mowed.
Alas! No one does eat the harvest!
O! The Extro children have hard lives.
From the *Song of Varloo*, Sleep Two

VARLOO SANG SOFTLY so as not to disturb Dougie
and his family, asleep in the shelter that was a dark
shape in the distance. It was strange to sing here
on the Surface. The words flew from her mouth

away into the empty sky. At home her words were never lost; they returned to her as echoes.

Varloo changed one word, then another, changed the whole verse and changed it back. Finally she was well satisfied. Indeed, she thought, there has never been a Spy who learned so much about the lives of Extro children.

Of course, neither had any other Spy been fed by an Extro child or sheltered by an Extro child in his *tree house*. Dougie had taught her that word and many others. Indeed everything Varloo knew about the Surface and the lives of the Extros were the things he had taught her.

Now he had taught her something else. The Song of LeRoy Shaeffer, which so abruptly did change the nature of her Mission. She had halfway hoped that something like this would befall her. Something to make her Mission interesting. She did not want her Song to be as dull as most of those she had studied.

Who could blame me for falling asleep when I was supposed to be listening to my tutors? Varloo thought. Except for Drasil's, the Songs of the Spies were dull as salamander soup.

Now she must needs come up with a plan, even as Drasil had done. And if, like Drasil, she could show that the danger had been great, that she had saved Hek from destruction, then the Druids might not judge her so harshly for consorting herself with an Extro. . . .

Varloo did not wish to think about the Black Chasm—whether it existed or not. And she did need more knowledge of the Surface world before she could devise the plan that would save Hek. Had it not taken Drasil several sleeps to acquire the knowledge she needed? Already Varloo had asked the helper to take her exploring, and they had fixed a time for the following sleep. For now she would think about her Song.

How to explain, for example, the spectacle boxes called TV, those that captivated the Extros and sapped their strength? She had not at first believed Dougie when he told her about them.

"Do you mean to say that you Extros do watch shadow pictures for hours all at once?" Varloo had asked Dougie when he brought dinner that evening.

"Sure." He shrugged. "It's fun."

"But what of singing? What of drama?" Varloo asked.

"Exactly," said Dougie. "That's what's so great about TV. It's got everything. Football too. *Rai-ders!*"

Varloo sighed. Sometimes this Extro was so cryptic. "But when do you yourself sing? Your family? When do you present your spectacles?"

"Me? My family?" Dougie looked confused. "Uh, never. I mean, most people aren't any good at that junk. So we watch it on TV."

Varloo had shaken her head, amazed. Presenting spectacles and singing—these had sustained the spirits of the Hekian people through the travails of adjusting to life underground, through the daily labor that life underground did require, through the maladies and infirmities that plagued them. Working the farms, fishing and hunting, running the mills and smithies, devising new means of transforming their world through alchemy, expanding and maintaining the lighting and dwelling systems, scouring and cleaning the walls and ceilings—the Hekian people did work long hours. Even the Druids and the children did their share.

Dougie had told her that the Extros also worked hard, particularly the children. But in so many ways, she saw, life on the Surface was very different. Hekian families, for example, lived in single rooms carved out of the cave walls. Extro shelters, on the other hand, were of magnificent size.

Here in this *neighborhood*—the closest settlement to the Hekian Portal—there were one hundred of these shelters, and each one incorporated a second called *garage*. The garage was solely for the storage of mechanized conveyances called *cars* or *minivans* or *SUVs*, depending upon their shape and size.

The Song of Brigid, Varloo's grandmother, had spoken of these conveyances, but Brigid had not known what words the Extros used for them. And from what the helper told her, Varloo believed there were now many more varieties of conveyance than there had been fifty years ago. Indeed it seemed to Varloo that many things on the Surface had changed in fifty years.

Dougie told Varloo that besides shelters, the neighborhood contained *streets* and *sidewalks*. The Story spoke of streets in the land across the water. But those had been narrow and paved with stones. Here the streets were black, wide and smooth, constructed to suit the size of the conveyances.

The Extros never did journey more than a few yards on foot. The helper had told Varloo this, and Varloo had observed it for herself. This sleep, as the bright orb had threatened, Varloo had heard the roar and smelled the pungent bitterness of many, many Extros departing in many, many cars, SUVs, and minivans. Even now, when most of the Extros did sleep, Varloo heard the occasional *swoosh* of a car on the wide black street beyond the helper's shelter.

Varloo began to compose another verse.

> **"The cars of the Extros are dizzying fast**
> **And cozy the cushioned thrones inside.**
> **O! The Extros never walk. . . ."**

Varloo paused. I wonder just how dizzying fast the cars are truly, she thought. How wonderful it would be to ride in one! Perhaps when we do go exploring . . .

Chapter Fifteen

DOUGIE HADN'T EXACTLY TOLD Varloo he'd take her exploring tonight. As a matter of fact, when she first asked him, he thought, Thanks but no thanks. It sounded dangerous. And from what he knew about Hek, it wasn't that nice a place. Varloo wasn't even polite. Maybe none of them was. Not to mention how they didn't laugh or smile.

But as he had lain in bed Monday, staring at the stick-on moon, something strange happened: Dougie began to like the idea. If he helped Varloo on her Mission, if the two of them saved her entire civilization, wouldn't he be a hero? He had kind of envied Varloo's getting to be a Spy. Even if Dougie never could tell anybody up here in his world what he'd done, the people of Hek would know. They would sing about him. They were always singing, Varloo said.

By the time he got to school Tuesday, Dougie had decided he'd show her around. But since he had that paper to write, he might as well learn what he could first. During library time, he asked Mrs. Wilkerson if it would be okay for him to write only about the "lost caves" and "man-eating trolls" under Spook Hill. She thought it was a great idea and suggested Dougie try to track down the origins of the superstitions by looking at early issues of the local newspaper.

"Do they have a website?" Dougie asked.

Mrs. Wilkerson laughed. "I don't think our local paper is quite so technologically inclined," she said. "You'll have to pay a visit to their office. It's on Main Street."

Of course, Mrs. Wilkerson didn't know Dougie had his own private source. He wondered how he was supposed to list Varloo in the bibliography.

After school, to his mom's amazement, Dougie announced he was riding his bike into Oak Hollow to do research on his paper. "Let me feel your forehead, honey," Mom said. "Are you feverish?"

Dougie rolled his eyes, and his mom grinned at her joke. "Seriously, I'm glad you've gotten interested in something," she said. "Tell me if you find out anything, okay? I'm working on the Spook Hill project too, you know."

"You are?" Dougie asked.

Cynthia Minners sighed. "That environmental

project? I've only been working on it nonstop for a month. Or didn't you notice?"

"Uh, well, I guess I've been busy."

"Hey, honey, one other thing," Mom said. "You haven't seen those old sunglasses of mine, have you? I thought I left them on the kitchen counter. I like to keep an extra pair in the car."

"Me? What would I be doing with your old sunglasses?" Dougie skirted a lie by asking a question.

"I can't imagine," Mom said. "But keep an eye out, would you?"

Chapter Sixteen

TWENTY MINUTES LATER Dougie was riding his bike down Main Street in Oak Hollow. The offices of the *Calaveras Republican* were next to the police station. He locked his bike to a parking meter, hoping that wasn't against the law.

"Do you have, like, a librarian or anybody?" he asked the woman sitting at a desk behind the front counter.

"Nope." She didn't look up from her crossword puzzle.

"Uh, well . . . is there anybody here who can help me find old newspapers?"

"How old?" She wrote in a word and smiled to herself but still didn't look up.

"Like a hundred and fifty years old," Dougie said. "More or less."

The woman turned her head to look at Dougie. "More than a hundred and fifty years ago there wasn't anything here 'ceptin' the Miwok Indians, and they didn't have a printing press," she said. "So you must mean less. Come on back. We got 'em bound in books—publisher won't pay for micro-film. No sense of history, that man."

The woman, who looked old enough to have known those original Miwoks personally, walked through the quiet building to a little room packed with filing cabinets and bookshelves. Dougie followed uncertainly. The woman's reaction was not real encouraging. This was probably a big waste of time. He didn't even know what he was looking for exactly.

"Oldest ones are these here." She reached up and yanked at the first of the volumes. A cloud of dust shook loose, but the heavy book, which was almost as tall as she was, didn't budge. Undaunted, she squared her shoulders, yanked it again, and almost toppled over when it pulled free. Dougie moved to help her, but she regained her balance and heaved the book onto a table for him. "Here y'go."

"Thanks."

"You got any bubble gum?" she asked.

"No," said Dougie, forgetting the piece he had stolen from Judah that morning. "I'm sorry."

"I don't want bubble gum, son. In my experi-ence, boys your age usually carry bubble gum, and

I don't want these pages getting sticky. These're the only copies we got. History—right here."

"I won't hurt anything," Dougie promised, but she was already heading back to her crossword puzzle.

Dougie opened the cover and looked at the stained and brittle pages inside. He didn't think he had ever seen anything so old before in his life. The first one proclaimed itself in inch-high type to be the "Inaugural Edition of The Calaveras Republican." Dougie was disappointed when he saw the date, August 1, 1855. From Varloo, he knew that Hek sent up a Spy only every fifty years. This newspaper had been published five years after the visit of Drasil in 1850. Dougie knew Drasil was Hek's most famous Spy, even though he didn't exactly know why. He kept looking. Even if these papers came later, there might be an article that mentioned Spook Hill.

He began to read. There were stories about the outlawing of water cannons (whatever they were), the construction of Oak Hollow's first church, and the arrival of somebody's sister from Minnesota. Three Chinese men were hanged for claim jumping, a punishment that horrified Dougie; the *Calaveras Republican* reporter who wrote the story

85

seemed to think it was perfectly fine. And there were several stories about spectacular fires. It seemed that whole blocks burned up every month.

A lot of it was pretty interesting. To think outlaws like Joaquin Murietta and Three-Fingered Jack had robbed and pillaged right here in Oak Hollow, which Dougie considered the most boring place on earth. It didn't even have a Taco Bell.

Dougie read and read and only noticed time was passing when the bubble gum woman checked on him. Finally, just as his stomach was beginning to complain that it expected a snack, Dougie found something—a little story at the bottom of a back page:

NEWCOMER SEEKS CLAIM TO NOTORIOUS KILLER MINE

by a Republican *correspondent*

Stick Creek—When it comes to James Skerdoff, who arrived earlier this month from the Empire State by way of San Francisco and the Stockton stage, folks in this camp are about evenly divided.

Half of them say he's crazy.

And half say he's a fool.

It seems Mr. Skerdoff is bound and determined to mine Spook Hill, and no amount of good, sensible talk from those with more experience and judgment will dissuade him.

"Cannibals and trolls?" Mr. Skerdoff scoffs. "It's no more than superstition! I am convinced by my own scientific reckonings that there must be a significant vein of gold in the quartz beneath Spook Hill. And I am the man to recover that gold."

Mr. Skerdoff has lately been surveying the western slope of Spook Hill with the idea of staking a claim there. The last claimant, as all the world knows, was young Mr. Asa Gonner, with whose grisly end readers are no doubt overfamiliar.

Here the article ended, but Dougie's curiosity was just beginning. "Grisly end"? Varloo hadn't said anything about that. Had the people of Hek murdered some poor gold miner?

He turned over a few more pages, then came to the end of the volume without finding anything else. His stomach was really grumbling now, but he had to find out if Mr. James Skerdoff had come to a "grisly end" too.

He closed the 1855 volume, returned it to its place, and tugged down the one for the following year. He hadn't been flipping pages long when he came to another brief story about Mr. Skerdoff. This one said he had finished his survey and staked a formal claim to the mineral rights below Spook Hill that, the *Republican* correspondent pointed out, was very unlikely to be challenged. As soon as the winter rains let up, Mr. Skerdoff planned to go at the hillside with pick and shovel. Dougie flipped ahead a few months. Sure enough, on April 15, there was a page 1 headline:

SPOOK HILL MINER DISAPPEARS

Did he run? Or was he eaten?

by a **Republican** *correspondent*

Stick Creek—Acquaintances of Mr. James Skerdoff, the newcomer who defied sound advice and endeavored to mine Spook Hill, report he has not been seen this past week, and some fear the worst.

Mr. Skerdoff, it will be recalled, arrived in the fall and soon surveyed and claimed the mineral rights under Spook Hill, the selfsame claim that lured young Mr. Asa Gonner to his grisly demise five years ago.

This past Sunday, while the devout improved their spiritual wealth in church, Mr. Skerdoff set out to improve his material wealth with pick and shovel.

"He said he thought there were caves up there, caves full of gold," reported Mr. Buckhorn "Shorty" Longworth of Stick Creek Camp. "There was no reasoning with him. I even went so far as to describe what was left o' young Asa when we found 'im—a sight I don't like to dwell on—and he laughed in my face."

* * *

The story went on, filling in a few details about Mr. Skerdoff's career before he came to California and adding I-told-you-so's from the miners at Stick Creek. Dougie just skimmed it. He was thinking about Mr. Asa Gonner's "grisly" demise—what did that mean anyway?—and wondering what had been left of him to find. The pictures in his imagination almost killed his appetite. Hurriedly, he turned more pages, expecting to find a gory obituary. Instead, in the paper dated April 22, he found this:

MISSING MINER LIVES!!!

Skerdoff claims he outran bloodthirsty ghosts, goblins

by *a* Republican *correspondent*

Oak Hollow—Word has been received that Mr. James Skerdoff, lately of Stick Creek Camp, has arrived in San Francisco, where, swearing never to return to California, he has booked passage on a steamer bound for the Isthmus.

Writing to Mr. Buckhorn "Shorty" Longworth, the would-be miner of Spook Hill described a harrowing and narrow escape from "pale and bloodthirsty shades" that "rose up glowing from the hillside like demons out of Hades."

According to the hastily scrawled letter, which Mr. Longworth was gracious enough to share with this correspondent, one of the apparitions was taller than the others and possessed of curly brown hair and a youthful yet fearsome countenance. Bereaved friends, including Mr. Longworth himself, say the description matches that of poor Mr. Asa Gonner, who died at the bloodstained hands of the supernatural beings that claim Spook Hill as their own.

"It was the poor boy's ghost come to warn away Skerdoff, sure as I'm flesh and blood myself," opined Mr. Longworth.

According to the letter, Mr. Skerdoff first arrived on Spook Hill filled with confidence in his claim and disdain for all those who had tried to scare him off. He set up his camp near a boulder veined with quartz, which he thought was auspicious, and commenced to work.

The now-chastened argonaut had worked for several days and was convinced he had come upon the entrance to a cavern, possibly one of extraordinary size, when he heard ominous noises. Believing them to be no more than the groaning wind, he continued to work that day until—just after sunset—the cataclysm came.

The poor man's mental state remains so agitated that, even now, his account of what happened next is confused. The apparitions were variously "ghosts and goblins dripping with blood," "terrifying trolls," and "fat and pale little people with ungodly eyes." They surrounded him, made an awful din, and hurled projectiles. When he attempted to use his sidearm, he discovered that it had jammed, an eventuality he blames on the supernatural powers of his assailants.

Exactly how Mr. Skerdoff managed to escape the deadly circle that surrounded him is not clear, but he took off at a run and is certain that the bloodthirsty beings chased him many miles before giving up their pursuit.

Once clear of them, the sadder but wiser miner wanted nothing more to do with Spook Hill, Stick Creek, gold, or California.

"I shall never be at peace until I am well away," he writes. "I would only admonish anyone else as foolish as I was to desist from all endeavors on that blasted hillside. No treasure is worth the horror I have experienced."

To Mr. Skerdoff's fervent plea, this correspondent can only add a vigorous "Amen." It is profoundly to be hoped that, now and forever, this dreadful place will be left the undisturbed domain of its even more dreadful inhabitants.

"Holy guacamole!" Dougie looked up from the page. "Spook Hill gets weirder and weirder!" He took out his notebook and copied down the parts about poor Mr. Skerdoff and the little he could figure out about the even less lucky Mr. Gonner. It was going to be a heck of a research paper, he was sure of that. But with his own personal "bloodthirsty goblin" in the backyard, would he live to write it?

Chapter Seventeen

Now must I too be a hero,
A hero who faces danger
And defies the Tenets that taught her.
From the *Song of Varloo*, Sleep Three

"LOOK, VARLOO." Once again the helper had climbed noisily into Varloo's shelter, leading her to suspect he had found out something more about Hek. Would he never be satisfied with the story as she told it? Why must he keep investigating for himself? These Extros were entirely too exasperating.

"Maybe I'm a wuss," he said, "but this is getting scary again. I mean, what do I know about you really? What was it Drasil did that made her such a hero? And what terrible thing did she do to Asa Gonner? Do you guys have a Song about him too?"

It was Tuesday night. Dougie had brought Varloo her dinner, and she was laying waste to her third *sandwich*. No, that was not right, Varloo thought. This was not *sandwich*. It was *hot dog*. She had much to be thinking about, but even so, one part of her mind considered the yellow spicy paste, *mustard*. She could not decide whether she did like it as well as she liked the red sauce.

Of course, there were more pressing matters. Life and death were two. She had some thoughts about how to thwart Mr. Shaeffer and his houses. But she was nowhere near to having a complete plan. And every minute brought the end of her Mission nearer.

Varloo's brain was so busy it seemed to bubble, and still the helper pestered her with questions.

Varloo did not answer at once but chewed silently on her hot dog. Dougie frowned and tugged on the brim of his black and silver hat. "I might have to turn you in," he said.

"Turn me in?" Varloo swallowed her last bite.

"Yeah, like tell my folks about you, or call the police. Look, I'm sorry. But I don't know if I can trust you. It's too weird."

"If you were to 'turn me in,' what would befall me?"

"'Befall' you?" The helper shook his head. "Oh, you mean like what would they do to you? I don't know. Put you in jail maybe. Till they thought of someplace else to put you."

"Then you must not do this turning!" Varloo said. "Helper, I am surprised that you should utter such a threat, especially now when you do understand the peril. Very well. To appease you, I shall sing of Drasil. And I shall sing of the Extro Asa Gonner. Then you will take me exploring. May we not borrow one of your family's conveyances? I long to ride in the coziness of that shiny black one, *SUV*. After all, we may have far to go. 'Tis important that we move with good speed."

"What are you, nuts?" Dougie said. "I'm a kid! Kids can't drive. Extros have Tenets too, you know."

"'Tis a pity," said Varloo. "Mayhap you know another fast mode of conveyance? I fear our feet would be too slow."

"Mayhap I do." Dougie smiled. "But first answer my questions."

Varloo wiped her mouth, patted her belly, and leaned back against her pillow. She must conserve her strength for the exploring that lay ahead. When she was comfortable, she spoke. "Drasil was the fifth Spy of Hek, even as I am the eighth."

"I know all that," Dougie said. "She was here at the time of the Gold Rush."

"Aye," said Varloo. "Now, you must imagine how it was for her when she commenced her Mission. The Spies before had found only the native people. There were few of them. Their ways did not pose any threat to us. But Drasil saw that the English cousins had come, bringing with them their wicked ways. With the coming of the English, all was changed."

"The wicked English cousins?"

"Mayhap you would call them pioneers, gold seekers—"

"But why do you call them cousins? Why do you call them wicked?"

"Helper, if you ask ever more questions, we shall have no time to accomplish our sleep's work. Now, hush."

Dougie hushed. Varloo went on. "Even before she commenced her Mission, Drasil was uncommon for a Hekian. She was independent, a quality that we of Hek do not value overmuch. The life underground requires hard work, cooperation, obedience to the Druids—"

"That and singing," said Dougie.

"The singing is also for the spirit," said Varloo.

Dougie nodded. "Go on."

"Drasil believed that the Extros' greed for gold would destroy Hek, and more, that this destruction was imminent. She knew that she must needs stop the Extros. She knew that she must needs act in haste. But she was on the Surface; she did not believe there was sufficient time for her to return home and consult with the Druids."

"So what did she do?"

"She devised a plan. And for the plan, she needed a helper—"

"Like me."

Varloo sighed. "I hope her helper did not interrupt so much."

"Sorry," said Dougie.

"She found a helper, and—wait. I shall sing to you. 'Tis part of the Song of Drasil:

> *"Now do I take a terrible risk,*
> *Defy the Tenets and our Custom,*
> *Consort myself with the Extro*
> *Asa Gonner*
> *Asa Gonner.*
> *O'r two sleeps have I watched him,*
> *Orphan from a distant land*
> *He calls this place Cal-ah-forn-yah.*
> *Here does he hope to find gold.*
> *My appearance does so amaze him*
> *Asa Gonner*
> *Asa Gonner.*
> *My golden necklace he covets*
> *And my story he does believe—"*

The helper had been shaking his head, which distracted Varloo from her singing. Irritated, she stopped and asked, "What?"

"That is so cool that you can just do that like that. Sing, I mean," Dougie said.

Varloo glared at him.

"Oh," Dougie said. "Sorry. Go ahead."

Varloo continued:

> *"My helper longs for riches.*
> *Gold flakes will buy him food,*
> *White sugar, he tells me,*
> *And beef*
> *O! How he does long for this beef!*
> *Gold flakes can I give him,*
> *Gold flakes and much more,*
> *If he returns with me to Hek*
> *And does pledge his troth to mine—"*

Dougie interrupted again: "Wait one hot minute!"

"Now what?"

"Does that mean what I think it means? That the terrible thing Drasil did to Asa Gonner was she married him?"

"He was my great-great-great-great-great-great-grandfather," said Varloo. "He sired seven children and introduced many new words and inventions to Hek. 'Tis considered a very romantic story."

Dougie made a horrible face. "Yeah, right—romantic," he said. "If you ask me, old Asa would've been better off as dinner!"

Nothing an uncivilized Extro could say would surprise me now, Varloo thought. Best to ignore him and go on.

> *"Now have I o'rstayed my Mission*
> *To gather all that we need*
> *To stage the awesome spectacle.*
> *To afright the greedy gold seekers,*
> *By stealth did we go to the butcher*
> *To gather up the entrails.*
> *By stealth did we go to the Chinese*
> *To gather up the fireworks*
> *That effect both noise and light*
> *Noise and light*
> *Noise and light . . ."*

Varloo took a breath and looked up at the helper expectantly.

"Don't stop!" he said. "It's just getting good. Now I see what you've been talking about. Drasil's Song says those old Hekians were going to put on a show, right? You told me you guys were good at that drama junk. And in the show I bet they pretended they were trolls and they offed Asa Gonner. To scare the miners away."

Varloo nodded. "Now do you begin to understand."

Chapter Eighteen

By TUESDAY NIGHT CURIOSITY was really gnawing at Judah. What was it Dougie did out there in the backyard? Was he all the way out in the tree house? But the idea of going out in the creepy zone to spy on his brother made Judah shudder.

Anyway, he was pretty busy with a secret of his own. A good one too.

The cat had recovered quickly after Judah had hauled her home, fed her, and warmed her up. When Judah checked her today after school, she had eaten all her food and was nosing around her new home, the cellar.

Judah had first thought of naming her Lucky, but just about everybody had a dog or a cat named Lucky. He wanted something more original. So he decided on Fortuna, which meant sort of the same thing, plus it sounded like a cat's favorite food, fish.

Judah liked having Fortuna. She was real friendly and seemed grateful that he had rescued her. She was always pushing her head against his hand so he would pet her, and today she rubbed up against his legs.

Judah also liked having something to take care of. He had gone to the library and looked up cats on Monday. There he found out how to look under the tail to find out boy or girl: girl. He also found out what Fortuna needed—a litter box, which he made out of a cardboard carton—and something soft to sleep on. For that he had brought down his own baby blanket, still kept in a dresser drawer.

The main trouble with cat ownership, as far as Judah could see, was the cost. He wanted to buy Fortuna some little catnip toys shaped like mice, but he was broke. He didn't have enough money for Skittles. Even his bubble-gum supply was getting low.

There was also Mom's allergy. He tried to get the cat hairs off when he came upstairs, but a few must have slipped by. Mom thought she had a cold, but Judah was pretty sure he knew better. Every time Mom sneezed, he felt bad.

Judah was hoping to look in on Fortuna before bed if he could. Luckily Dad was watching a Giants game on TV, and Mom was working upstairs. She had been working a lot lately.

Judah drank the last of the Count Chocula–

sweetened milk, put the bowl in the sink, then walked out the kitchen door and around the house to the cellar steps. It was dark back here, but he had swept yesterday so the steps weren't so dirty anymore. As he descended, he felt the air grow damp. Quietly he turned the knob and went in.

Fortuna must have been waiting. Meowing, she came toward the door and tried to slither around Judah's legs.

"Hey, kitty, what's up?" Judah pushed the door shut before she could get past. "Are you trying to escape or something?"

Chapter Nineteen

Spying days done,
Heroism past,
Drasil the woman lived long enough
To become old and mistrusted,
Her ideas too strange to be believed.
Was she ever frightened
By the gravity of duty?

                                  From the *Song of Varloo*, Sleep Three

VARLOO WAS WAITING for the helper to speak.

"Go on," he said. "It's great."

"Alas, 'tis the end," Varloo said. "She never did finish the verse."

"You're kidding! How come?"

"'Twas at that moment the searchers did find her," Varloo said.

"What searchers?"

"The Council had grown troubled when Drasil did not return at the appointed time. They dispatched three searchers. As the three approached her shelter, they saw that an Extro came out. This did naturally alarm them, and they hid nearby.

"At first they feared that Drasil was dead, but

103

then they saw her. When they realized she was not held against her will, that she had consorted herself with an Extro, the Druid who led the searchers ordered that she be executed on the spot."

"What?" Dougie looked alarmed. "I thought you told me Hekians were peace-loving!"

"Peace-loving, aye," said Varloo. "Most of us are. But even in these times a few are of a warlike disposition." She thought of Herne, who had wanted to fix a weapon to the Portal rock so that any Extro who came near to it would be destroyed. Then there was Fen, the youngest of the Druids and one of her tutors. He once had threatened to blast another council member during a disagreement. Most Hekians believed both Herne and Fen to be foolhardy, but all did agree on the need to defend Hek.

Varloo went on. "'Twas Drasil's good fortune—and Hek's—that the other searchers were more temperate. They convinced the leader that the knowledge she had gained as Spy must be shared with the Council. She must therefore be brought back to explain herself. Believing that Drasil and the Extro would be asleep, the searchers waited till dawn and then raided the shelter."

"But they weren't asleep," Dougie said.

"Indeed not. They were hewing to Extro hours, sleeping in Surface darkness rather than in daylight. And there was something else too. Asa Gonner possessed a gun. At that time the Hekians did not possess any weapon so powerful."

"Do you have guns now?" Dougie asked.

"Oh, aye. All manner of guns. We Hekians are a fearsome people and should not be trifled with by mere—"

"Oh, come on, Varloo," Dougie said. "You're faking."

Varloo sighed. She wished it were easier to fool him. "We do have weapons," she said. "But they are a bit different from those that you call guns."

Dougie grinned as if he thought only guns could be powerful weapons. Varloo hoped he never did have to discover the truth.

"Asa and Drasil heard the searchers coming," she said. "When the searchers opened the flap of the shelter, Asa had his gun cocked and ready. Drasil was sitting in the corner where she had been composing her Song."

"Pretty intense! Then what happened?"

Varloo paused. "I would rather not say."

"Why?"

"'Tis embarrassing."

"Well, okay," said Dougie. "I hope they have lasagna in the Oak Hollow jail."

Varloo was indignant. "After all that I have told you—"

"Okay, okay. I won't really turn you in. But come on? Please? What happened?"

Varloo resigned herself to telling the rest, scandalous as it was.

"Well," Varloo said, "at the time Asa Gonner was no more than a barbaric Extro."

"Like me," Dougie said proudly.

"Aye, well . . . to him, the three Hekians, clothed in long robes and shaded spectacles, did appear humorous. Indeed he laughed. Soon he was so overcome he could not properly aim his gun."

This made Dougie laugh as well. Varloo crossed her arms and waited. She had feared such a reaction.

"Have you now finished?" she asked finally.

Dougie wiped his hand across his mouth as if he could wipe away the smile. "Yes," he said. "Please continue." But he cackled twice more before he was quiet.

"For their part," Varloo said, "the searchers were confounded. They never in their lives had seen an adult reduced to laughter. Their moment of confusion gave Drasil her chance, and hastily did she explain the danger. Thus did she convince the searchers to spare their lives. Then, once they had returned to Hek, Drasil persuaded the Council to stage the spectacle."

"Right—the spectacle! So how did that work?"

"My Ancestors did paint their faces and dress in frightful costumes. They used the fireworks to attract the miners' attention. As the audience was gathering, they acted out the terrifying sacrifice of Asa Gonner on the Portal rock. By the time the miners were sufficiently near to see clearly, Asa Gonner had disappeared back into Hek as had the 'trolls.' All that remained were the blood, bones, and guts of some unfortunate cow."

Dougie looked disappointed. "They didn't pretend to eat anybody?"

"That must have been an embellishment appended by the miners," Varloo said. "Or mayhap by the Extro Bards in their chronicle."

Dougie shook his head. "Well, even if they didn't eat him, it's a good story. But you know the best part?"

"What?"

"The laughing part. I mean, you see it, don't you? It was laughter that saved Hek."

"No! 'Twas Drasil! 'Twas the spectacle—"

"Wrong." The helper's voice was certain. "I mean, I see how the spectacle was important. It kept people away from Hek until James B. Skerdoff came—"

"Asa Gonner was permitted to make forays to the Surface at that time. It was thought to be necessary for his health since he had so lately come to live underground," said Varloo. "'Twas fortunate, for 'twas he who spotted this Extro, Skerdoff. Another spectacle had to be staged straightaway."

"But don't you get it?" Dougie said. "There wouldn't have been either of those spectacles if ol' Asa Gonner hadn't laughed. He would have shot those searchers—*blam-blam-blam*—and then Drasil couldn't have gone back home or reported on the gold miners at all."

Varloo considered what the Extro was saying. 'Twas contrary to all the Druids' teaching. But in truth she recognized the sense in it. Varloo was feeling a bit uneasy in her mind. All her life she had learned that Extros were stupid. And yet this Dougie Minners did not seem to be so.

Of course, she never could admit any of this to him. "'Tis preposterous!" she said. Then, to change the subject: "There is one more thing I should tell

108

you. 'Tis a thing that treats with you and me."

"You and me?" Dougie said. "How's that?"

"Drasil lived a long life. As an old woman, shortly before she died, she did call the Druids to her. She said she had something important to impart. A prophecy."

"A prophecy? That's like a prediction?"

"Aye." Varloo spoke slowly. "She said the Extros would always be greedy. 'Twas their character to be so. She said that even were the greed for gold to pass away, it would be followed by some other, mayhap for land. In that time another Spy would be called on to save Hek, even as Drasil had done. And that Spy would do well to study her Song."

"Wo-o-o-ow . . . so you mean . . . you think . . . like, you might be that Spy? And I might be your helper?"

Varloo nodded. "The Druids did not believe her. An old woman's raving, they said."

"But what do you think?" Dougie asked her.

Varloo shrugged. "I do not know."

The helper considered for a minute. Then his eyes got wide, his face flushed red, and he shook his head violently. "I won't do it! No way! I'm sorry, it's nothing personal, just I'm way too young, and I hate girls, and—"

At first Varloo could not puzzle out the reason for the helper's agitation. Then, abruptly, she understood. She could not laugh. So she coughed. Then she protested, "No, helper, no. I did not mean that. I do not wish to be betrothed to you. This do I vow!"

Dougie still looked upset, but he said, "Well, okay, then. I guess."

"Helper, if 'twill ease your anxiety, I shall tell you something more: I am already betrothed. To my near age-mate, Kalvis."

"You're kidding!" Dougie said. "But you're just a kid!"

"In recent times all Hekian marriages have been arranged by the parents for the children," Varloo explained. "In this way we have learned to ensure that the offspring are healthy and fit. And Kalvis does please me well. He does look comely, and I am told he is kind."

"You're told?" Dougie said. "You mean you don't even know him?"

"He does stand beside me during the singing on Festival Days," Varloo said. "But in truth, I do not know any of my near age-mates. The Spy is special, and so she must be kept apart."

"But what about friends?" Dougie asked.

Varloo sighed. "The Spy has no friends."

Chapter Twenty

THEY WERE SPEEDING down a hill, and Dougie had to shout to be heard over the whoosh of wind and whir of wheels: "I can't believe I let you talk me into this!"

"Aye," Varloo hollered. "The SUV would have been a good bit faster and more commodious. But what do you call this again? This thing on which we sit?"

"Bicycle!"

"Of such a thing did my grandmother sing, but methinks I am the first Hekian to ride one!"

Dougie wished he could see her face. She sounded happy. Was it possible she was smiling?

Dougie might have been happy himself—if only Suzy Shaeffer had had a better bike than this old clunker pink one. He never would have chanced the embarrassment of riding such a thing except in the middle of the night, when absolutely nobody was out on the road. Still, it was lucky they had Suzy's bike since there was no way to ride two on

Dougie's. Suzy's basket, with a cushion wadded up inside, had become a passenger seat.

"Hey, Varloo—"

"What?"

"Did you hear the one about the chicken that crossed the playground?"

There was a pause. "No, helper."

Dougie already had tried a couple of jokes on her. No luck getting her to laugh.

"He wanted to get to the other slide," Dougie yelled. "Get it? Slide? Not side?"

Varloo's answer was polite. "I am sure I would enjoy this joke . . . were I an Extro."

Uphill now. Dougie pedaled hard. There were plenty more jokes in the library. He had forty-eight hours till Varloo's Mission was over, forty-eight hours to get her to laugh.

It was still Tuesday night or, more accurately, Wednesday morning. After he had heard Drasil's story and answered a few million more questions, Dougie had returned home from the tree house, put his pajamas on over his clothes, brushed his teeth, and climbed into bed.

"Have you ever done anything heroic?" he asked when his dad came in to kiss him good-night.

"Heroic?" Dad said. "Well, I put up with you and Judah every day. That's pretty heroic."

"Aw, Dad, that's not what I mean," Dougie said. "Like running into a burning house to save somebody's dog? Or . . . helping a spy save an entire civilization, or . . . junk like that?"

"Save an entire civilization?" Leo Minners scratched his chin. "Well, there was the time this kid on my street was aiming sunlight at an ant colony. You know, through a magnifying glass. And even though he was a lot bigger than I was, I told him I didn't think it was very nice."

"What did he do?"

"Ignored me and kept right on," said Dougie's dad. "But it turned out okay. Instead of the anthill, he burned a hole in one of his sneakers. He had to run home and put his foot under the sprinkler."

"Is that true?" Dougie asked.

"Mostly," said his dad. "Now, sleep tight."

But Dougie didn't sleep. He waited. Mom's office light was still on. He and Varloo couldn't leave till he was sure she was in bed. Trying to stay awake, he thought about Jon Gruden, the Raider coach. Everybody knew he slept only two hours a night. Dougie yawned and wondered how in heck he did it.

Finally the light went off, and the house was quiet. Dougie had removed his pajamas and stuffed them and his pillows under his covers as a decoy. He put on his Raiders cap, tiptoed down the stairs, and raced out of the house.

Now he was riding toward Oak Hollow with Varloo perched in front of him. She was still wearing Mom's old sunglasses. It was pretty tough for him to see around her, let alone steer. And he kept worrying about her stupid long dress getting caught in the spokes.

"Let us look for the bulldozers of LeRoy Shaeffer," Varloo had suggested. She had got it into her head that maybe they could stop the project if they stopped the machines. Dougie said sure because it was better than any of her other ideas; and besides, there were other reasons to take her into town.

Like he wanted to stop at the twenty-four-hour minimart and buy her some new sunglasses.

And he thought she really ought to do some exploring. She couldn't learn all a Spy should know about "Extros" from sitting in a tree house, even if she did have an especially intelligent Extro helper.

The parking lot at the minimart was deserted when they coasted in. Through the windows they saw only a single clerk at the counter. "Do you want to come with me?" Dougie asked Varloo. "You could pick out your own sunglasses. And it would be new material for your Song."

Varloo looked through the plate-glass windows. "Will that Extro recognize that I am a Spy?"

"Are you kidding?" Dougie asked. "A guy with a job like that sees weirder stuff than you every day."

"*Minimart.*" Varloo obviously liked saying the word. "Let us proceed."

Once they were through the doors, Varloo shaded her eyes with her hand and never stopped swiveling her head to take in the sights. For the first time Dougie totally understood the meaning of another one of Mom's phrases: "kid in a candy store." That was Varloo in a minimart.

"The light is bright—bright as the sun methinks," Varloo said. "But mayhap my eyes are adapting. And as the Spy I must needs observe what is here. 'Tis awe-inspiring!"

She visited each display, asking, "This? What is this?" She was particularly excited when she recognized any of the foods Dougie had brought her. "Behold the goldfish crackers!" she cried. "I never knew there were so many, not on the Surface entire!

"But why does everything hum so, helper? Why is the light here tinged with green? What are these things encased in glass? And these—are they edible also?"

Dougie couldn't keep up with her questions, but he did his best to explain the refrigerator and freezer cases. He also noticed that the clerk had looked up from his hunting magazine to watch them. Dougie hadn't counted on Varloo's being quite this excited. Time to buy her some sunglasses and get going.

"Here, Varloo, look." Dougie pointed at the revolving rack of sunglasses. "These are good ones, don't you think?" He grabbed plain black ones that seemed like something a Spy would wear.

"O my Drake!" Varloo ignored his choice, took a pink and black zebra-striped pair from the rack, and held them up to her eyes. She didn't dare take Mom's off to try the new ones now, though, Dougie realized. The store was too bright.

"I do find these wonderful!" she breathed.

"You're kidding," Dougie said.

Varloo looked hurt. The clerk was still watching them.

"You're right; they're perfect," Dougie said. "Half price too. Can't imagine why. Come on."

He had ten dollars in his wallet, and on sale the glasses were only $2.69, including tax.

"May we not have one of these?" Varloo pointed at the Slim Jims. Dougie just wanted to leave, so he said sure, and of course Varloo asked for one of those and a couple of the other things too. Next thing Dougie knew, he had spent the rest of the ten dollars on snacks. The clerk never said a word.

In the parking lot at last, Varloo insisted on putting on her new glasses. "How do I look?" she asked Dougie.

What could he say?

"Wonderful." In the dim light he couldn't be sure, but he thought he saw a near smile on her lips. "Varloo, come on," he said. "Let's get out of here."

There was no place but the basket for the snacks, so they stowed them beneath the cushion. Dougie's heart didn't slow down till they were back on the road and beyond the spill of the minimart lights.

Chapter Twenty-one

WHERE IN OAK HOLLOW would a Spy's helper find bulldozers?

Dougie didn't have a clue. So he steered the bike toward the center of town. Except for music and lights from its three bars, the main street was dark and quiet. He and Varloo had ridden less than a block when she commanded, "Halt!"

Dougie did. He guessed he was getting used to her ordering him around.

"What is that?" Varloo pointed at the Cadillac Saloon.

"Hmm . . . I don't know exactly how to explain it. Only grown-ups go there. They drink beer, and there's music—"

"A public house," said Varloo.

"Pub, you mean? Yeah, that's what they call it in England, I think. How did you know that?"

"We have public houses in Hek," she said.

"Get outta here! Do the grown-ups drink beer and dance?"

"They drink fern tea and sing."

Dougie shook his head. Those Hekians didn't have very fun ideas about fun.

"Let us proceed," Varloo said.

"Yes, ma'am." Dougie saluted and pushed off from the curb. "That's the courthouse, which is really old, and over there's the newspaper office— you know, where I went to do the research about man-eating trolls." He pointed at the building as they rode by. "And that's the police station. . . ." His voice trailed off. "Uh-oh."

A police car had pulled out of the station's garage and into the driveway. Now it turned up the street—right behind the bike. Dougie had a bad feeling it wasn't legal to ride somebody in front of you in a bike basket.

Varloo turned her head to look back over Dougie's shoulder. "What is that conveyance?" she asked. "I do not like the red lantern it does flash."

"Red lantern?" Dougie looked back himself. "Oh, no, Varloo. We're sunk! That means he wants us to stop."

"We cannot!" said Varloo.

Dougie was torn. He was ordinarily a law-abiding kid. But no way were the circumstances ordinary. How could he possibly explain Varloo to a police officer? He couldn't risk their being taken into the station, his parents being called, any investigation of his mysterious friend with the outrageous sunglasses. Dougie didn't like it much, but he had only one choice. And luck seemed to be on their side.

Across the sidewalk to the right was a walkway between two buildings. It was narrow, but Dougie thought the bike could make it. He turned sharply, nearly knocking Varloo off the basket. Then he pedaled hard. His elbows knocked against the sides of the buildings, but a second later they shot into the street on the other side. Dougie steered right, then left at the next corner and right up a steep hill that—with the extra weight up front—almost killed him. The street ended in a T, and he stopped to catch his breath. Below them blared a siren.

"Where are we?" Varloo whispered.

"I don't know exactly," he whispered back. There was a row of darkened little houses on the downhill side of this narrow street, a steep hillside on the other. The siren sound faded, but now he heard a car, and it seemed to be getting closer. Then, all of a sudden, he saw headlights at the bottom of the hill they had just climbed.

"Shoot!" Dougie looked right and left—dead ends in both directions. They couldn't dump the bike and run; Varloo wasn't fast enough. Hide in a driveway? Stay put and hope it wasn't the police at all?

There was one other choice.

"Hold on!" Dougie said, and as the headlights approached, he aimed the bike right toward them and took off.

"Do you wish to—," Varloo yelled, but she inhaled the rest of her question.

In a flash Dougie had steered around the oncoming car and was making the turn at the bottom of the hill. With Varloo in front of him, he didn't see a bump in the road and hit it squarely, bouncing the bike into the air and back to earth— oh, that hurt!

But Varloo held tight, and Dougie kept pedaling, even though his leg muscles burned like fire. Up another hill, and another—the clunker bike had only three gears. Finally he stopped, panting.

Had that car been the police? He had gone by it too fast to get a good look.

Dougie was pretty sure it was a crime to run from the police—not to mention whatever it was they wanted him to stop for in the first place.

"Helper, mayhap 'twould be better—"

"Just a second," Dougie said. "I'm thinking." Dougie reached under his Raiders cap to scratch his head. By now he was thoroughly lost, so he rolled to the corner to see the street sign: OLD CALAVERAS ROAD. Was that the one that paralleled the highway? He looked up at the sky, found the Big Dipper and the North Star. If he followed this road east, it ought to lead to the other end of his subdivision. Anyway, they couldn't go back toward town.

"Helper!" Varloo didn't like being ignored.

"What? Sorry?"

"Mayhap we should abandon our search for bulldozers this sleep. Deliver me back to my tree house."

Dougie couldn't believe it, she was so clueless. "Varloo, the police were chasing us! Do you know what would have happened if they caught you? Obviously, I'm taking you back to the tree house! I just hope nobody spots us on the way."

Varloo didn't answer immediately, and Dougie felt bad for being rude. Finally she said, "I am sorry, helper. I know how hard you have worked this night, how difficult has been the pedaling of this *bicycle*. I have heard the exertion in your breathing. I am grateful."

Well, Dougie thought, this was a switch. Varloo had never told him she was grateful for anything— not even when he rescued her from the bank of Stick Creek. Before, she had always acted like she deserved whatever he did for her and more. Now he felt a little embarrassed.

"Don't mention it," he said. "Let's just get you home."

Few cars traveled the old road now. Dougie didn't expect to see any this time of night. But about halfway back, he heard something behind them. The police again? Dougie looked over his shoulder, and that was when the worst happened. A gust of wind caught the Raiders cap, knocking it from his head. *Squeee-al* went the bike brakes as Dougie steered onto the packed-gravel shoulder. The car, which wasn't the police at all, whooshed by.

"Why do we stop?" Varloo demanded.

"Why do we stop? I lost my Raiders cap! Hop off now, quick. Before it blows away."

Dougie threw his leg off the bike and jogged back to where he thought the cap had fallen. The weeds beside the road were tall and green from the spring rain. It could be lost forever in there, Dougie thought desperately.

"Are not hats abundant here on the Surface?" Varloo came up behind him. "You may obtain for yourself another. What about these *police*? I wish to return to my tree house."

This was more like the old Varloo, and Dougie felt a surge of anger as he pushed back the weeds and tried to see. It was Varloo's fault he had lost his ball cap. He wouldn't be out here in the middle of the night, in the dark, in the wind, running from the cops, if it weren't for her. He felt another gust. The Raiders cap probably had blown to Stockton by now. . . .

"'Tis there, I do believe." Varloo pointed. Dougie could barely make out the shape where it lay yards away up the road. He had been looking in the wrong place. Without Varloo's see-in-the-dark eyes, he never would have found it.

But Dougie was too mad to appreciate anybody's eyesight. He trotted down the road, picked the cap up, shook the dust off, and put it back on his head. Without a word the two climbed back on the bicycle. Fifteen minutes later Dougie came to a street he recognized—Prospector. He turned left and soon was racing by familiar houses. He turned into his driveway, cut onto the lawn, then coasted around the garage and into the backyard. His leg muscles felt like overboiled noodles.

Varloo hopped down. Miraculously her new zebra-striped sunglasses were still in place. "Helper . . ."

"What?"

"The foods. From minimart."

Dougie was afraid that if he said anything, it would be mean. Looking for his ball cap, he had felt all the excitement of the night turning into anger. He had his cap back, but the anger wouldn't go away. So, without a word, he took the cushion out of the basket. The Slim Jims and licorice whips looked fine. The chocolate bars were squished city.

Varloo didn't seem to care. She took them all eagerly, then hesitated. "Do you wish to share with me, helper?"

Dougie's anger dissolved in surprise. What was with the new and improved Varloo? "No, that's okay," he said. "I can eat that junk whenever I want. But you've only got a couple more days before you have to go home."

"Aye," said Varloo. And again Dougie noticed that she didn't sound like herself. Did she feel bad about something? He wanted to ask her. But it could wait till tomorrow. It was so late, and somehow or another he had to get up for school. He was pretty sure he could never get by on two hours a night.

"You have rescued me now three times," Varloo said, "from the creek, from the girl who would intrude on my tree house, and this night from police."

Dougie felt embarrassed. "Aw . . . it's okay."

"Alas, 'tis not," she said, without explaining. "Rest you peacefully now. And thank you."

Dougie watched Varloo turn and waddle away. Pushing Suzy's bike toward the garage, he thought about another of his mom's sayings: "Will wonders never cease?"

Then he looked up and saw something that scared him worse than the police car ever had: The light was on in his parents' bedroom.

Chapter Twenty-two

DOUGIE TIPTOED INTO THE GARAGE with Suzy's bike, thinking maybe he could sneak back into bed, pull the covers over his head, and claim he had been there all along. But that fantasy disintegrated when he saw a light go on in the kitchen and heard the back door creak.

"Dougie? Is that you? *Dougie!*"

"Yeah, Mom. . . . Hi."

For the next few minutes Dougie stood blinking in the kitchen while his mom shelled him. But it wasn't her anger that got to him; it was all the crying mixed up with it. Dougie could feel his face turning raspberry red. He even wiped off a tear of his own. Somewhere in the middle of the barrage Dougie's dad came down the stairs, rubbing his eyes, and then Judah came down too. Mom didn't even pause, just shot Judah a look, and he went back to bed in a hurry.

"And what do you have to say for yourself, young man?" She had asked this six times already, but now she was out of breath and paused as if she expected him to answer.

Dougie had read somewhere that the best lies are the ones closest to the truth. "I was, uh, doing research," he said, "for my cave paper."

Dad snorted. "Pretty lame, son."

"Do you want to try again?" asked his mom, sniffling.

"I wanted to see the trolls on Spook Hill for myself," Dougie said. "Trolls only come out at night. They can't see in the sun."

This sounded good to Dougie, plus it was sort of true, but his parents obviously weren't buying. "So I guess I'm grounded, huh?" he said, hoping that would put an end to the questions.

"Grounding isn't half bad enough," his mom answered, and she seemed dangerously close to starting the whole crying and yelling thing over again.

"Yes, you're grounded. For a month. And no TV either," said Dad.

"What about Nintendo?" Dougie asked, and knew right away he shouldn't have brought it up.

"That too," said his mom through a tissue. "No Nintendo."

Dougie shambled upstairs after his parents.

Their door was closing when he remembered something. "Mom?" he said.

"What is it?"

Her sunglasses had been in his pocket. He pulled them out, and they looked a little flatter than they used to. "Uh, I found these," he said.

She gave him a very puzzled look, took her sunglasses, and closed the door.

Back in his own room Dougie was so tired he collapsed into bed without even taking off his Raiders cap. But he didn't fall asleep right away. He was thinking about the sacrifices a hero has to make.

Chapter Twenty-three

Every time Dougie sat down at his desk Wednesday morning, his eyes drooped, then closed. Mrs. Wilkerson must have asked him five times if he wanted to go to the nurse. Even Suzy Shaeffer acted worried.

"Wake up, Dougie!" She nudged him when he drifted off during reading time. "I've got soda in my lunch. Sugar and caffeine. You can have it if you want."

"That's okay, thanks." He yawned. Half a minute later she had to nudge him again.

After lunch Dougie revived a little. It wasn't soda but chicken nuggets and chocolate milk that did it. Wednesday afternoon was when Mrs. Wilkerson's class got to use the lab where the computers were linked to the Internet. Dougie had one more piece of research to do on the cave paper. There was a chance the Internet would help.

Dougie sat down at the computer table, moved the cursor to "search" and typed in "D-R-A-K-E." It was what Varloo said when she was really happy, or really upset—the same way he said "holy guacamole." Something in the back of Dougie's mind kept trying to make a connection between that word and the other things Varloo had told him about Hek. But he couldn't quite do it.

Back came the search response: twenty-three matches. Most of them had to do with Nick Drake, the singer, or Drake University, and then there were some towns named Drake too.

There was one more match. Drake, Francis.

Dougie woke right up. Holy guacamole. That was it! How could he have been so stupid? Hadn't he had a whole year of California history?

The entry the search engine found wasn't a source Dougie had ever heard of. It was some weird thing called *Frank's Encyclopedia of Lore and Legend*. Mrs. Wilkerson had told them a thousand times you couldn't trust everything you read on the web. But it was worth a click to see what came up, wasn't it?

Dougie clicked and read:

SIR FRANCIS DRAKE, THE MAN AND THE LEGEND
Born the son of a farmer in 1540, Francis

Drake became one of the wealthiest and most revered men of the Elizabethan age by virtue only of his boldness and intellect. Much of Drake's remarkable life is well documented, but there are persistent legends about him that never have been verified.

One in particular stands out. If it were true, it would change our understanding of American history by introducing new candidates for the title of the first English colonists in North America. These colonists settled not on the east coast of the United States but in what is now California. And like their counterparts in the "lost colony" of Roanoke Island, their fate is unknown.

The middle of the sixteenth century was a time of great religious antagonism and disorder in England. Not long before, King Henry VIII had broken with the Catholic Church and created the Protestant Church of England. His daughter Mary, who was to assume the throne in 1553, was a devout Catholic who wished to return England to Catholicism.

Francis Drake was the son of Protestant parents in the north of England, where most people were Catholic. When he was a child, his family was one of several forced to flee their land in fear of religious persecution.

Now here is where the historical record gets murky. Apparently among the neighbors of the Drake family was a man called Uther—

"Uther!" Dougie said it out loud; Mrs. Wilkerson looked over.

"Yes, Doug?"

"Nothing. Sorry. Just found something interesting is all."

"Your zeal for research is admirable. However . . ."

"I'll be quiet. Sorry," Dougie said.

—man called Uther, whose religious beliefs were suspect. Drake's family escaped with their lives, but Uther was not so fortunate. He was burned at the stake for heresy. According to the legend, the young Drake witnessed this hideous spectacle and never forgot it.

Burned at the stake? So could that be the "Ancestors' ordeal" Varloo talked about? That meant her ancestors were English people, and maybe to her the pioneers were too. No wonder she had called them wicked English cousins.

Twenty-two years later—in 1579—the Protestant Queen Elizabeth was on the throne, and Drake was a celebrated privateer, naval captain, and explorer. In June of that year, on his way to becoming the first Englishman to circumnavigate the globe, Drake landed on the coast of the land he called Nova Albion, which is now Northern California.

Drake had set sail with five ships from Plymouth, England. Four of the ships sank or were abandoned before they reached California. Again this is part of the historical record. But legend has it that another ship weathered the stormy seas and made it to California with Drake that summer.

Like the *Mayflower* forty-one years later, this ship carried religious exiles seeking the freedom to engage in their beliefs without per-secution. Supposedly these exiles were the followers of the martyred Uther, whom Drake remembered from childhood and helped now that he had the means.

Drake would have had a second reason to help the exiles. He had developed a great hatred for Spain after having been captured by the Spanish in the West Indies some years before. Spain claimed California. Drake knew that a colony, even a colony founded by heretics, eventually might help secure the land for England.

Who was Uther? And what were his heretical beliefs? Some say he and his followers were Druids—

"Druids!" Dougie clapped his hand over his mouth as soon as he said it. "Sorry, Mrs. Wilkerson."

But it was amazing how it all fit. Uther was a Druid, Varloo had said. And what else? Something about how he unified old religious beliefs? Something about alchemy? Then there were the guys who still ran things in Hek. Varloo called them Druids too.

Dougie looked back at the screen.

—were Druids, among the last adherents of the ancient religion that had prevailed throughout Europe before the time of the Roman Empire. Uther also may have studied alchemy, the pursuit of the connection between the natural world and the spiritual world. It is no longer fashionable to link scientific inquiry and religion, and most people today discount alchemists as tricksters. In fact, however, alchemical inquiry was pursued throughout most of the world for thousands of years, often by great thinkers and philosophers. Even Sir Isaac Newton studied alchemy, and some of the foundations of modern chemistry and modern medicine may be traced to alchemical origins.

As for the Druids, it was they who, about three thousand years ago, constructed the massive stone monument in southern England now known as Stonehenge. This was probably a giant open-air temple, but the stones were placed in such a way that it also could be used to predict the positions of the sun and moon in relation to the earth.

In other words, the monument was a calendar that told the seasons and, with less precision, the days of the month. The people who designed and built this structure were not only brilliant engineers but also sophisticated and keen observers of the natural world.

The legend of the band of exiles brought to California by Drake has startling historical implications. For one thing, it flies in the face of the widely held assumption that all traces of Druidism had been wiped out by the sixteenth century. What may be even more interesting to Americans is that it would mean the first English colony in the New World was not the one founded by Sir Walter Raleigh at Roanoke, Virginia, in 1587, but that established in Northern California by the followers of an ancient religion.

That was the end of the article. Dougie scrolled back to read the top part again, the part about no one knowing the fate of the Druid colonists.

As of now, that's wrong, Dougie thought. There is one person who knows what happened to them. And that person is me.

Chapter Twenty-four

BEFORE THE BUS DOORS even opened, Judah was jogging down the aisle.

"Slow it down, buddy!" the driver said. "Baseball team can't afford to lose its star player."

Judah said he was sorry, then grabbed the railing on the side of the door, vaulted to the curb, and sprinted up the sidewalk toward home.

Dougie and Suzy were still in their seats, putting on their backpacks.

It was Wednesday afternoon, and Judah had only fifteen minutes before he was picked up for baseball practice. Barely time to get a snack and visit Fortuna. The cat had been acting so weird lately. Judah was afraid she must be lonely, but he didn't know what to do about it.

"Hi, Mom!" Judah hollered from the kitchen.

"Judah?" She was in her office, of course. The meeting about the Spook Hill project was tonight. She'd been getting ready for it forever.

"Be right there, Mom." He grabbed an apple

from the bowl, bit into it, then ran back outside, around the house, and down the cellar steps. He'd be upstairs again before Dougie even made it home. His brother was incredibly slow.

Judah knew he had to slip into the cellar carefully, not open the door too wide. Every time he visited her, the big gray cat tried to slither her way between him and the doorjamb. He had the feeling she waited there, planning her getaway.

But why?

Didn't he treat her well? He had bought her those catnip mice, washed the car to earn the money for them. Maybe she wanted better food. But he already fed her the most expensive brand the minimart carried.

"Hey, kitty," Judah whispered. "Hey, Fortuna, how ya doin'?"

Today the cat had a new strategy. As soon as Judah edged into the dark room, she jumped up and tried to climb his body like a tree. The sharp claws surprised him: *"Yo-o-o-ow!"* He tried to shake her off, dropped his apple, and the door swung wide. Before Judah knew it, Fortuna was bounding up the steps and heading for freedom.

Judah ran after her, but she had a good head start. He reached the top of the steps in time to see her disappear into the shrubbery.

Then he heard his mom calling, "Mrs. Browne is here, honey! Time to go to practice!"

Shoot. He couldn't look now. He would just have to find Fortuna later.

Chapter Twenty-five

DOUGIE WAS SO EXCITED about his incredible Internet find that he forgot all about being in trouble. He couldn't wait to talk to Varloo. He was so happy he even waved to Judah, riding off to baseball practice in Mrs. Browne's minivan.

Then, from the kitchen, he heard his mom's voice: "Dougie?"

And it all came back to him. "Yeah, Mom?"

"Front and center, young man. I want to talk to you."

Dougie took his time on the stairs. When he got to Mom's office door, it was half open, but he knocked anyway. "Did you crawl?" she asked. "Never mind. Sit down."

The floor of Mom's office was a maze of stacked papers and file folders. Dougie had to weave in and out to get to a chair. When he sat down, a wave of exhaustion washed over him.

"You want to try again?" Mom reached for a tissue from the box on her desk. "I was hysterical last night—I admit it. But can you blame me? Now I want to know the truth about where you were."

Dougie wished he were a little kid with little-kid secrets. Then he could tell his mom and he would feel better. But the secret he had now he couldn't tell anybody. It wasn't only that he had promised Varloo. It was also that he could see for himself. It wasn't the sixteenth century anymore. Nobody got burned at the stake. But Dougie could imagine the whole thing: reporters, TV cameras, Spook Hill becoming a tourist attraction. For sure, if the Hekians wanted to be left alone, they needed to stay a secret.

"I've told you everything I can, Mom," he said. "I'm really sorry. I didn't mean to scare you to death like that."

Mom sneezed.

"Bless you," Dougie said.

Mom dropped the tissue in the wastebasket and sniffled. "Look," she said, "if you're in trouble, maybe I could help."

"I'm not in trouble exactly. But if you want to help, you could unground me."

"No way."

"Didn't think so." Dougie half smiled, and so did his mom. They seemed to be stuck. He was about to ask if he could go do his homework, a question he had never in his life asked before, when he happened to notice the title on the file on his mom's computer screen: "Preliminary Spook Hill Environmental Assessment."

"What's that about?" he asked her.

"Dougie." She sighed. "It's not as if we don't live in the same house. Besides, I told you the other day. I have been working on the Spook Hill project for a month plus."

Dougie defended himself. "I knew you were busy. But what are you doing on it exactly?" Then he had a horrible thought. "You're not working with Mr. Shaeffer, are you?"

"Not hardly," she said. "You know he and I don't agree about much. I'm on the other side, the Foothill Defense Fund. FDF. We're trying to convince the planning commission to deny him the permits. They meet tonight."

Dougie couldn't believe it.

Varloo's ideas for stopping the project had been ridiculous. First she had suggested a spectacle like those they put on in Drasil's time, but Dougie had said no way would it work. People now were so used to the special effects on movies and TV, there was nothing he and Varloo could do that would scare them.

Then she had said they should kidnap Mr.

Shaeffer, which Dougie thought would be hard on Suzy and her mom, not to mention illegal, not to mention impractical.

Finally Varloo had had this vague idea about stopping the bulldozers. Dougie could think of a million reasons why that wouldn't work either. But he didn't have the heart to nix any more of her ideas. In the end it didn't matter. They never found bulldozers.

Anyway, all this time Mom had been working on her own plan to stop the project. And Mom's sounded a lot more reasonable.

"That's terrific, Mom! Are you going to do it? Stop him, I mean?"

"Truthfully?" Mom said. "I doubt it."

Dougie slumped. "Oh. Why not?"

"We need to show the commissioners that there's something worth saving on that hill," she said. "There's nothing wrong with building houses, after all. People have to live somewhere. A project's bad only if it's in a place where building houses does damage. We suspect Spook Hill is that kind of place. Unique."

Unique is the word, all right, Dougie thought. "So how do you convince the commissioners?" he asked.

"We need hard evidence. And I'm afraid we won't have enough time or money to collect it."

Dougie remembered something he had read in the first newspaper story about Mr. Shaeffer's project. "Collect hard evidence," he repeated. "You mean, like say, maybe there really are caves under that hill—you mean, like a bat? That lives in them?"

Cynthia Minners nodded. "A bat might be just what we need. But there's no question about the caves, Dougie. We had a geologist out there all morning, and I talked to her a few minutes ago. She hasn't finished her work yet, but caves are definitely there."

Geologist? Out there all morning? On Spook Hill? Dougie's face must have shown his horror because Mom asked if he felt all right.

He told a partial truth. "I'm sleepy, Mom. But can I ask you another question? What was the geologist doing?"

Dougie tried not to shudder as Mom explained that the geologist was using a backhoe—a kind of small bulldozer—to dig up samples of earth. The samples would help determine if the ground was firm enough to support houses.

"And is it?" Dougie asked.

"Seems to be," said his mom. "The caves are quite far below the surface."

Dougie hoped they were far enough below that the backhoe hadn't hurt anything—or anyone. It was more important than ever that something be done—done fast—to protect the Hekians. Dougie thought a plan was forming in his brain, but he was so tired he couldn't tell if it made any sense. And he needed to know more about this planning commission business.

"Mom," he said, "at that meeting tonight, what will the commissioners do?"

"Probably say they need more information," Mom said. "But FDF—that's us—spent almost all the money we've got on the geologist. I don't think we can afford the studies we need."

Chapter Twenty-six

Now do I leave my tree house,
Begin the journey home,
Chastened by my failure,
Humbled by the truth.
From the *Song of Varloo*, Sleep Four

VARLOO UNCLASPED from around her neck the gold necklace, emblem of the Spy. No longer did she deserve to wear it. Her rucksack she had already packed—the map, the food packets, Osi's lead, her matches, her clothing, the folded shelter. Her hands were shaking as she placed the necklace on top of her belongings and tied the flap with an awkward knot.

Varloo was giving up.

All her life long she had been told she was special and, obedient as any Hekian, she had believed herself to be special.

The Spy. The first daughter of the first daughter. The daughter of a Druid.

Even after Osi did drown and she did fall, even after her rescue by an Extro—still she had believed her Mission would be a triumph and her Song would be fine.

And later, when she learned of the peril that now did threaten Hek, she had been confident that she was the new hero, the one foretold by Drasil.

The doubts had begun to form slowly. First she had recognized that the helper was not stupid as Extros were supposed to be. This had led her to ponder something else: With their fast conveyances, their magnificent shelters, their delicious foods, were the Extros really stupid at all?

Then came last night, the exploration. It was a turning point. First, she realized how little she did know of the Surface world. Second, she realized how much she did rely on the helper—for safety, for knowledge, for her very existence here.

The truth was painful to bear: Dougie Bartholomew Minners was a better hero than she.

Varloo had not slept this day. Mayhap 'twas ill advised to eat all the food of minimart at once. Afterward her stomach was troubled, which at first did keep her wakeful. Later it was not her stomach but the cogitations of her mind. One plan after another for the salvation of Hek did she contemplate. One plan after another did she discard.

The bright orb was descending in the west when she did see and comprehend the meaning of the omens at the departure ceremony, of Geber's harshness, of her mother's and grandmother's troubled faces. She was not up to the task. She had not applied herself sufficiently to her training. She was not clever enough. All had expected her to fail. All except Varloo herself.

What was there left for her to do here on the Surface? She would return in disgrace to Hek and sing to the Druids the Song of the Extro LeRoy Shaeffer. Mayhap the Druids would be sufficiently wise to stop the building of the Extro shelters. But this she doubted. Were not they the ones who had taught her that all Extros were stupid? They knew far less of the Surface world than she.

As Varloo slipped the straps of the rucksack over her shoulders, a tear ran down her cheek. She remembered one of the first conversations between herself and the helper. "Do you cry?" he had wanted to know. And she had answered, "Indeed we cry. Should we not have feelings?"

Through her tears Varloo bade good-bye to the tree house that had cocooned her. Then she stepped backward from the platform and felt with her foot for a rung. The first one was loose, and she stumbled backward. The contents of the rucksack shifted, but soon she had righted it and herself. Steady again, she descended in haste. Was there

149

not a noise from the direction of the Minnerses' shelter? The helper always came to see her after his family's dinner. It still was early, but she would not chance a meeting. 'Twould be too painful for her in the changed circumstances. She was not only a failure but also a coward.

Chapter Twenty-seven

JUDAH MINNERS KNEW every story about Kit Carson in the library. Now, for the first time, Judah had his own quarry to track, and he wondered how ol' Kit would have handled it. It hadn't rained in a while, so there wouldn't be paw prints anywhere. And cats buried their stuff neatly—not like disgusting dogs—so there'd be none of those clues either.

Fortuna might just come back on her own, Judah thought. But the way she'd been acting lately, he sure couldn't trust that she would. So, when he got home from baseball practice, he slammed the back door and headed toward the shrubs where he had last seen her.

Judah couldn't call his cat without alerting his family, so the search was strangely silent. For a while he flipped rocks over and poked plants, not sure what kind of sign he was looking for. It's too bad I can't ask my blisterbrain of a brother to look, Judah thought. Dougie was out here all the time. But you couldn't trust a secret with Dougie.

Judah looked toward the creepy zone. He sure hoped Fortuna hadn't gone that way. He hated it back there where they didn't mow, just let the weeds grow wild. There were all sorts of creeping things, not to mention poison oak and burs and foxtails. Still, a cat wouldn't mind spiders and snakes. He ought to have a look, a quick look.

Hesitantly Judah walked out beyond the forsythia, scanning weeds for cat or clue. The closer he got to the oak where the tree house was, the more slowly he walked. Tarantulas, rattlesnakes, ticks, thorns—yuck! His skin seemed to crawl with all of them. He was about to turn back when something fluffy on a blackberry bush caught his eye. He bent down to examine it—long gray cat fur!

Fortuna had come this way!

Judah was proud of himself. He bet even Kit Carson might've missed a tiny furball.

The light was fading, but when Judah stood up and looked toward the oak again, he saw dinky white things on the ground underneath it. They looked all wrong among the acorns. Cat teeth? Hating every step, he went to investigate. They weren't teeth; they were pills. Now he saw a plastic bottle too: Tylenol.

What was that doing here? Could the pills have

fallen from the tree house? What else was up there? Judah didn't like the idea of climbing that rickety old ladder. It was probably a mass of splinters too. But Kit Carson wouldn't have hesitated. So Judah mustered his courage, climbed up, and looked in.

Judah didn't know what he had expected. Dougie's hungry girlfriend maybe? But there was nothing inside, not even dust. Judah was looking down over the wall when a ray of late-afternoon sun made something near the bottom of the ladder glint gold. Now what?

Judah climbed down carefully and picked the thing up.

What in the world! How would some old chain get way out here? It wasn't his mom's, he knew that. And it must not be worth anything. Still, it was sort of pretty, and he had just the place to keep it safe.

Chapter Twenty-eight

Varloo was missing. When Dougie went out with her leftovers, she was gone, and so was all her junk. Had she gone back to Hek early without even saying good-bye? Why would she do that? Was she mad at him for something? She had been so strange last night, but strange-nicer, not strange-meaner.

He couldn't figure it out.

Dougie looked at the black and silver Raider alarm clock by his bed. It said 2:30 A.M., but that was what he thought of as Raider time, just a little different from everybody else's. Probably it was more like 2:45. He had fallen asleep right after Mom came home, but his dreams had been terrible, and now he was awake again. Wide awake. He was worried about Varloo. And about Hek. He desperately wanted to tell Varloo his plan.

Mom had come home from the planning meeting with news. Those commissioners had talked a long time but finally come to the conclusion she expected. They wanted more information.

"So Mr. Shaeffer can't build anything on Spook Hill until there's a study of what plants and animals will be affected," Mom explained.

"Animals like bats," Dougie said.

"Exactly," said Mom. "But as I told you, the trouble is time and money. Shaeffer's got a lot of clout with the commission, and he wants to get moving. So they've put the project on a fast track. The county will start its study immediately—Friday most likely—and the commissioners meet again in two weeks. We can't afford to hire our own biologist, and the county won't be thorough enough to find everything we think is up there."

I sure hope they don't, Dougie thought. Aloud, he said, "Two weeks isn't long. But what if something lucky happened? Like somebody just happened to find evidence—proof—that there were rare bats in those caves?"

"That would be terrific," Mom said. "But what hero do you have in mind for the job?"

The clock said 2:36. Dougie rolled over onto his stomach and listened to the crickets chirping. Then he rolled onto his back and stared at the swaying shadows of trees on his wall. It was no use. He couldn't stand it. He was grounded for a month,

155

and if he got caught this time, he'd probably be grounded till his twenty-first birthday. But he had to do it. He didn't care so much about being a hero anymore. He just wanted to protect the people who lived in Hek.

For the second night in a row Dougie slipped down the stairs. He didn't know how long he would be gone, so he grabbed his backpack and stuck a water bottle and a package of Varloo's favorites, Oreos, inside. Once safely beyond his backyard, he called out, "Varloo?" But the name disappeared in the sky.

Dougie ran on. A dark shape swooped over his head, too small for an owl—a bat. That was a good sign, wasn't it? Maybe it was one that roosted in the caverns of Hek.

Breathing hard, Dougie jogged up the hill to the overlook, then jogged down again, almost to the creek. That was when he saw something, something extremely peculiar. He had gone to his first wedding last summer, and some of the guests had danced in a conga line. The weird procession ahead of him on the path looked like that, a munchkin-size conga line.

What in the heck?

Chapter Twenty-nine

Found and lost
Lost and found
Mayhap my fortunes do change.
From the *Song of Varloo*, Sleep Four

THE SEARCHERS HAD INTERCEPTED her even before she had reached the creek. Seeing them, Varloo had presumed she must have failed in some hitherto unsuspected way. Was it possible she had mistaken the number of sleeps till she was due to return?

Her grandmother, Brigid, reassured her. "'Tis nothing you have done, child. 'Tis what did happen in Hek that alarms us. We feared for your safety here on the Surface. For that reason did the Druids take the extraordinary measure of sending searchers. Methinks I never have been so glad to see anyone as I am to see you now. But tell me, where is the sacred cat?"

Varloo found that she also was glad to see her grandmother and even the other two searchers, Maria and the young Druid Fen. After the strangeness of the Surface world, their very familiarity was comforting, and some of Varloo's anxiety lifted. 'Twas harder to imagine the end of Hek, of her very world, in their presence. Mayhap there was still a chance. . . .

"The sacred cat is lost," she said simply. "I shall sing of her in due course, with your permission. But please, what is it that has happened in Hek?"

Brigid explained. On that very sleep, Wednesday, there had been a disturbance. A portion of the ceiling near to the Vent did collapse. Unluckily Geber himself, unable to sleep, had happened by on a sojourn. He had been partially buried, but the sentries did uncover him before he suffered ill effects—ill effects beyond a momentary loss of dignity at least.

In truth the trouble was not the cave-in. Repairs already had been undertaken. The trouble was its suspected cause: The sentries believed they had heard some kind of machinery that apparently had penetrated from the Surface into Hek. The implications were frightening.

"What did you see when you came to the Surface? Was there any sign of Extros near the Portal?" Varloo asked.

"The ground had been disturbed," said Maria. "But we found nothing more."

Now that the searchers saw that Varloo was

safe, they wanted her to tell them: Did she know what might have caused this? Would there be more danger to Hek?

Varloo knew from Dougie that the Extro LeRoy Shaeffer would not begin constructing his houses till summer. It would not be of any great importance if she waited one day before singing of this to the Druids.

"I do not know precisely the meaning of this cave-in," she said, "but I know of matters that may pertain to it. On our return to Hek, I shall sing of them."

But now she was so very tired. She had been awake so long and had walked so far. She had had so little to eat. Could they not rest? As the Spy she was not due back till the awakening from this very sleep.

Varloo's request caused some dispute among the searchers. Fen desired to return with all haste. Varloo had never liked Fen much. He was the same hotheaded one who had threatened to blast a fellow council member. Besides this, he was her Story tutor, and in part she blamed the tedium of her lessons on his tuneless singing.

"Geber did equip him with a blaster," Grandmother confided to her. "He is supposed to protect us."

Maria, the other searcher, agreed with Brigid and Varloo that rest would be wise. Outnumbered, Fen had been persuaded.

Not without some fumbling did they erect the three shelters. The task was unfamiliar to all but Varloo, who had been tested on it as part of her training. 'Twas just before first light that Varloo and her grandmother entered the shelter they were to share. Varloo slipped the rucksack from her shoulders so that she could unpack what she needed. Its flap was not tied shut, she saw. She must have knotted it poorly in her haste to depart the tree house. Then she realized something else. Something terrible. The gold necklace of the Spy— had it not been on top of her belongings? Where was it now?

"Is something wrong, child?" Her grandmother noticed her frantic searching.

Varloo already had the cat to explain. She was unprepared to explain the necklace yet. Thank Drake no one had noticed she did not wear it.

"No, Grandmother. I only am hungry. I was looking here for something to eat."

"I have a fish bun," Grandmother said.

"Thank you, Grandmother."

Varloo thought once again of the Song of the

Black Chasm. If it were not a myth, surely the place had been reserved for her alone, a Spy who not only had consorted with an Extro but also had lost the gold necklace itself.

She was nibbling unhappily on the bun—tasteless compared with the foods of the Extros—when she heard a familiar sound.

An ornery and complaining sound.

A wonderful sound: a cat meowing to be let inside.

"O my Drake! 'Tis Osi!" Varloo pushed open the flap, and in strutted the sacred cat, nose and tail raised high.

Surely 'tis an omen, Varloo thought. And, for once in my Mission, an omen that does bode well.

Chapter Thirty

DOUGIE WOKE UP WHEN the sun shone right in his face. One ear hurt—it turned out using a rock for a pillow wasn't such a hot idea—and there was still a wad of tasteless bubble gum in his mouth. It was lucky he hadn't choked to death in his sleep.

He sat up stiffly, spit out the gum, and peeked around the toyon bush that hid him. The tents were still there, not that he had doubted they would be. If he knew one thing about Hekians, it was how much they hated the sun. No way would they risk going out until night.

The conga line on the path had been Hekians— three grown-ups and Varloo. All were about the same height and wore wide-brimmed hats, sunglasses, and heavy robes like the guys who live in churches and chant.

So the Druids had sent searchers, just like in Drasil's time, Dougie thought. That couldn't be good. Maybe Varloo was their prisoner.

Dougie trailed the Hekians. Worried as he was,

he could see why Asa Gonner had laughed uncontrollably when he saw them. They walked like grounded ducks. Watching them pitch their tents was better than *The Three Stooges*.

Now Dougie unwrapped another one of Judah's bubble gums and stuck it in his mouth. Breakfast. Why not? Wasn't he hidden behind a bush in the woods when he should have been home getting dressed for school? But he had come this far. If Varloo was in trouble with her own people, he had to help her. Besides, it was important for her to hear his plan. I have to stay here, he thought. Somehow I'll find a way to talk to her or send her a signal or something.

As Dougie watched, there was a commotion inside Varloo's tent, and then a big gray cat came bounding out. That must have been her meow Dougie had heard earlier. Next he heard Varloo's voice: "Osi!" Dougie crouched down in case one of the others came after the cat. A minute passed. He looked again. The cat stood a few feet away from the tents, sniffing the air. Then, as if she'd been searching for him all along, she turned toward Dougie and trotted to his hiding place.

"Hello, cat," he whispered as she pushed her face into his hand, demanding to be petted. "Is your name Oh-see? Hey, maybe this is like one of those Lassie things."

Dougie had watched enough old TV shows that he had no trouble believing in animals who rescued humans in distress. Come to think of it, Varloo had told him about a cat, a special one she had brought with her from Hek. But that cat had drowned, hadn't it?

Still, this cat had come out of a Hekian tent. Maybe it was special too. "Is Varloo in trouble?" After the weird events of the past few days, talking to a cat seemed normal.

Osi turned around and stuck her tail in Dougie's face. Maybe that was a cat's way of saying "trouble." "Look, is it like with Drasil? Does she need to be rescued—yes or no?" Osi blinked her big yellow eyes and purred. "She does need to be rescued!" Dougie said. Cat wasn't such a hard language. He only hoped Hekians were heavy sleepers.

By now the sun was well up in the sky. It must be about eight o'clock, time to leave for school. He felt awful when he thought of his poor mom being awakened with the news that once again he wasn't in his bed. If she had been hysterical the first time, what would she be now? But he couldn't think about his parents now. He had to concentrate on what he was doing.

The cat, her message delivered, had curled up to take a snooze in the shade beneath the bush. The Hekians would be asleep too. It was time to get heroic.

Chapter Thirty-one

DOUGIE CROUCHED LIKE a runner at the starting line and took off in a zigzag pattern, tree to bush to tree, toward Varloo's tent. He told himself he wasn't afraid, not really, but every time a stick cracked under his sneaker he stopped, and every time he stopped he heard his heart pounding.

He was only a few steps away, close enough that a sound from inside the tent—snoring?—was louder than his heart, when he remembered Varloo had told him the Hekians had weapons—nothing so bad as guns, but something. He ought to have a weapon too. Heroes always did. But what?

Dougie looked around but saw nothing promising, only acorns and pinecones. The Hekians might be short and round, but they wouldn't be scared of pinecones. Then he had an idea. Only an arm's length away stood a sprawling bush with lots of shiny green leaves. He knew he might be making a big mistake, but those leaves had never bothered him before. So he broke off a branch and waved it over his head like a club. He was as prepared for battle as he ever would be.

Dragging the weapon, Dougie dropped to the ground and crawled the last few feet to the tent's entrance. He was just about to lift a corner when a small boot came through the opening and stepped on his outstretched fingers. Dougie sucked in his breath to keep from howling, then raised his head to see who was on the other end of the boot.

"'Tis you, Dougie," Varloo whispered. "I heard a noise. What do you do there on the ground?"

"I'm rescuing you again," he whispered back. "Could you move your foot?"

"Sorry," she said, and did. "I do not require rescue. Have you seen the sacred cat?"

"The one from your tent? She went over there. Can't you come out for a minute?"

"I feign would speak to you as well," she said. "But the searchers must not see us together." She seemed to hesitate, then decide. "Come. Let us go from here quickly."

Dougie stood up without a word and followed as she did her best approximation of running. Dougie noticed she stayed in the shade of the trees and kept one hand over her eyes, hidden behind the pink and black zebra sunglasses. She must be hurting in this sunlight, he thought. But on she goes. She really is tough. A few minutes later they could hear the creek. Panting, Varloo came to a stop in the shade of a boulder.

"What is that you hold in your hand?" she asked when she had caught her breath.

Dougie had forgotten he was still carrying it. "This?" He pointed the branch at her and tried to look fierce. "It's my weapon."

Varloo looked puzzled.

"It's a chemical weapon," he explained. "Poison oak. Anybody I touch with it gets all itchy."

"Are you all itchy?" she asked.

"It never bothers me. Just other people."

Varloo looked skeptical. A ray of sunlight slipped over the rock; she cringed and stepped back into the shade.

"Do your eyes hurt?" he asked.

"'Tis no matter," she said, but he knew she was faking.

"Look, do you want my ball cap? I lent it to you last time."

"With my minimart spectacles, there is no need. Besides, I know how much the cap does mean to you."

"Pride and poise," he said.

168

"Aye, Dougie. Pride and poise."

Dougie knew that any minute the Hekians might wake up, come looking, and find them together. On the other hand, they were so slow. . . .

"Where were you?" he said. "Why did you leave like that?"

Varloo explained. As best he could understand it, she had been embarrassed when she found out she wasn't perfect. So embarrassed she was scared to see him again.

"Varloo, that's crazy!" he said. "And it was mean too. I was worried about you. I couldn't sleep!"

"Worried?" Varloo repeated.

"Friends don't just run out on each other because they're embarrassed." Dougie was getting mad. "You're supposed to know your friends will forgive you for junk. You're supposed to know they don't expect perfect."

"Friends?"

Dougie had used the word without realizing it. Was that how he thought of Varloo? The Spy? The tough, stuck-up girl who came from a whole other civilization? Was she his friend?

"Well, yeah," Dougie said. "Friends. What else do you call it when you spend days together talking and helping each other and having adventures and sharing things? I mean, that's friends."

Before Varloo turned her head away, Dougie saw a tear slide out from under the outrageous sunglasses. Now it was his turn to feel embarrassed. It was almost to change the subject that he broke the big news. "I have a plan," he said, "to save Hek."

Varloo wiped her cheeks. "What plan?"

"It's easy," he said. "All we need is a bat."

Dougie gave her the abridged version of everything his mom had told him. Varloo said there had been a cave-in, which must have been the geologist at work.

"There are still difficulties," Varloo said. "How to deliver a bat to your mother. How to explain to the Druids that you and I—"

"That we're friends," Dougie said simply. "I know it's not all figured out yet. But it's like I learned from my mom . . . and the Oakland Raiders: Where there's life, there's hope. Besides, nobody's got a better idea."

Varloo seemed to consider. "Mayhap 'twill work at that," she said. "Osi, the sacred cat, did return. 'Twas an omen, methinks."

"Cat? That big gray guy? Yeah. I talked to him." Dougie was about to tell Varloo the story, but he heard a noise behind him. A noise like someone moving through the trees.

"Shh." Varloo put her finger to her lips and motioned for him to follow. They walked fast and quietly toward the creek. When Dougie looked back, he thought he saw something move, but he couldn't be sure.

"Why are we running away?" Dougie whispered.

"I do not know for certain what Fen would do if he saw us together," Varloo said. "He has an evil temper."

"Are you thinking of Drasil and Asa?"

Varloo shrugged. "Let us cross the creek. Methinks 'twill take the searchers much time to do this. We shall be safer on the other side."

"The bridge is this way," Dougie whispered. They walked upstream toward the downed tree. When they got there, Dougie said, "I'll go first and hold your hand."

"I will go first, and I do not need anyone's hand."

Dougie was almost relieved to hear Varloo speak that way. She must be feeling more like her old self.

"Can you swim?" Dougie asked.

"There will be no need."

It took a while for Varloo to maneuver herself

and her ridiculous robe up onto the tree trunk. Her progress along the trunk was wobbly, and Dougie hoped he didn't have to dive in and save her. How deep was that water anyway?

Dougie spit out his bubble gum and unwrapped a new piece as he watched her make her way. Pride and poise, Varloo, he said to himself. Pride and poise.

Halfway, a branch obstructed Varloo's path, and she teetered. Dougie stuck the new gum in his mouth and chewed furiously. But a few steps later, looking surprisingly sure of herself, Varloo jumped down on the other side.

Dougie had walked across this tree a dozen times. He couldn't help showing off by scrambling up quickly and trotting along. He even made a little leap over the broken branch in the middle, and that's what did him in. Dougie had no time to grab or even to think before he tumbled into the shockingly cold water, which splashed over his head and into his eyes and nose.

"*Aaa-aaaa-ccccchhh!*" he sputtered when he bobbed up. But he caught only one breath before the water washed over him again. Calm, he thought, stay calm—don't panic. But his body wouldn't obey. His arms and legs thrashed instead of treading water, and the current swept him into rocks and fallen limbs. It seemed as if a painful eternity passed before one of Dougie's feet hit the creek bottom and reflexively pushed his body upward till his head was abovewater. Then the other foot found a hold, and suddenly he was standing in the middle of the creek.

Dougie wiped the water out of his eyes and shook his head to clear his ears. When he looked around, he discovered he was only a few yards downstream from the broken tree . . . and the "deadly" waters reached only to his waist.

Dougie was disgusted. I thought I was gonna die, and it turns out I'm in a kiddie pool, he thought. Worse yet, I had an audience. His vision still blurry with water, he looked for Varloo. There, standing on a rock a few feet away. She was bent double and shaking all over.

Was she overcome with relief that he was saved? She was not. She was laughing.

Chapter Thirty-two

DOUGIE NEVER GOT TO ENJOY his triumph. He barely had time to realize he had finally made Varloo laugh—okay, by making an idiot of himself—when there was a terrible *boom*, and something whizzed past his head.

"'Tis a blaster!" Varloo cried. "Make haste, Dougie. O my Drake, that Fen is a fool! What was Geber thinking?"

She wasn't laughing now.

Dougie had never heard of a blaster, but he got the idea. Expecting to be shot any second, he splashed his way out of the creek and through the mud, then bulldozed through the brambles on the bank.

"We must get ourselves into the thick of the trees," Varloo said. "He cannot blast what he cannot see."

Dougie didn't understand entirely, but he grabbed Varloo's hand and ran with her, propelled by the thought of that awful noise. Finally, when their breath gave out, they stopped. They were bruised, scratched and—in Dougie's case—drenched.

"We shall spend the day here," Varloo announced.

"The whole day? Here? But my clothes are soaking wet!" Dougie pushed dripping hair out of his eyes. "Besides, the brush is so thick we can hardly sit down."

"Aye, 'tis a shame about your clothing," said Varloo. "But the orb will make the Surface hot this day. Soon you will be dry again."

Dougie wanted to take his shirt off and wring it out, but he was embarrassed in front of Varloo. So he shook himself, feeling a little like a dog, and put up with the damp, icky feeling of wet cloth against his skin.

"'Tis the brush that makes it safe for us here," Varloo explained. "Fen will not follow across the creek. And even if he did, he could not take aim to blast."

"I thought there weren't any guns in Hek," Dougie said.

"The blaster is not properly a gun. Not like the guns of the Extros. It works on the principle of air and niter."

"Air? You mean like a peashooter?"

"I do not know this peashooter. But the projectile of the air blaster is as deadly as the bullet of your gun."

Now Dougie realized how ridiculous his poison oak branch must have looked to Varloo.

"We shall spend the day here," Varloo repeated. "Mayhap we shall clear a space to rest. Then, at the conclusion of this sleep, at the hour appointed for the Spy's return, you and I shall return to Hek together."

"I'm going to Hek?"

"Aye," said Varloo. "I see no other way."

Chapter Thirty-three

'Tis fitting, methinks,
That as I return
To my home away from the sun,
The world has turned all
Topsy-turvy
My first friend an Extro boy.

From the *Song of Varloo*, Sleep Five

"Listen," said Varloo. "Do you hear it?"

"Sort of a creaky, whirring sound?" Dougie said. "Yeah. So that's the staircase?"

Varloo nodded. They were standing together at the Portal rock. It was still dark, but the light would come soon. It was the appointed time for her return.

Dougie had wanted to go home this day and leave a note for his parents—something—so they would know he was okay. Varloo had wanted to return to find Osi. But they realized that neither was possible. Fen and his blaster were out there somewhere and not to be trusted.

So Dougie and Varloo had stayed in their wooded hiding place, talking and eating Oreos while

Dougie's clothes dried on his back. Once or twice they had heard noises nearby, but never did they see a searcher. The day had passed in conversation. How grateful she was that he had followed her, that he had declared his friendship and they had spent this time together. How foolish she had been to leave without saying farewell! There was strength to be gained in friendship, she saw. She had not been such a very good Spy, but her mind was no longer so troubled. Indeed she was hopeful. Mayhap the two of them still could save Hek.

They talked and talked. 'Twas surprising that there were still more questions to ask and answer—about Hek and about the Surface.

She did not understand this Internet he spoke of, but she saw that he had learned much from it. He knew about Drake and the colonists. So she explained about the governance of Hek—the Druid leaders, the Bard storytellers and teachers, the Ovate healers and priests.

Dougie had known about bards. But Ovate? "What a weird word," he said.

Varloo told him that her mother was one. In certain cases she was as powerful as a Druid.

"How many Hekians are there?" he had asked.

"One thousand and three, unless Iona by now has been delivered of her baby," she said.

"How many came over with Drake?"

"There were one hundred and seventeen that left from England. But some died on the journey, and others during the early years underground," she told him.

"Why did they go underground in the first place?" he wanted to know.

"Fire had taken Uther from us, and fire is a form of light. Odin believed Uther's martyrdom to be a signal from the gods that we should banish ourselves from light. Someday, says the prophecy, our people will return to it."

"Come back up here, you mean?" Dougie had asked. "To live?"

"Aye," said Varloo. "But not soon. The signs are not auspicious."

They had spoken of personal matters too. He told her the secret of the hat he always wore, of the mysterious game called football, and of the magical incantation "Pride and poise." She in turn told him something she had never told anyone—how lonely it was to be the Spy.

"I'm kind of a loner myself," Dougie said. "Suzy was my friend, but then she discovered horses. It's not so bad, though, right? I hang out in the woods a lot. Well, I guess you know that."

Now, as she listened to the staircase descending,

Varloo realized that these moments were her last on the Surface. Only extraordinary necessity would bring her back here, as it had brought her grandmother today. For the sake of Hek, she did not wish for such necessity. . . . But did she wish never to return?

'Twas too difficult a question.

Varloo took a last look at the spreading oak that symbolized Hek, at the waning moon, at the stars in the sky. Then she breathed deeply the sharp, dry, cool air that had seemed so strange five sleeps ago.

"What are we waiting for?" Dougie said. "Do we have to move the rock, or is it automatic too?"

Varloo wondered that he was so eager. For her own part she was nervous. That was why they were waiting. She knew well who would be there to receive the Spy on her return. Her mother. Geber. The principal Bard. The council members—all except for Fen. In their hiding place she and Dougie also had discussed the moment of their appearance in Hek, more particularly of his appearance in Hek.

Still, she was nervous.

"Varloo? Earth to Alien?"

"Aye, Dougie. Let us proceed. You do follow."
Varloo knelt at the base of the boulder, dropped her

chin and rolled her body forward. As she did, her shoulders pressed a hidden lever in the rock, and a trapdoor was lifted. Over she somersaulted, emerging upright on the landing at the top of the forbidden staircase.

Ah! The darkness! So soothing to her eyes. And the damp smell was cozy. She enjoyed the familiar sensations as she removed the wonderful minimart spectacles and arranged her gown. Then she waited for Dougie.

And waited for Dougie.

O my Drake! she thought. Did I explain insufficiently how 'tis done? But here was a noise, and here came the Raiders hat and—

Thud. Dougie fell through the trapdoor after his hat and sat down hard at the top of the staircase. *"Ow!"* he complained. "Next time, Varloo—"

"Next time?" She smiled. In less than one sleep her lips had grown accustomed to forming that shape. Now she would have to discipline herself again. She was home.

Dougie smiled too. Then he stood up, rubbed his tailbone, and looked around. "Holy guacamole," he said. "Is it ever dark in here! And they—the Druids and all—they're down there?"

"Aye, Dougie. Give me your hand. I am your helper now."

Chapter Thirty-four

DOUGIE BLINKED FOR A LONG time after his eyes had adjusted. He was at the bottom of the staircase now, standing next to Varloo, and he couldn't believe what he was seeing.

In fact he couldn't believe he was here. Varloo had convinced him a long time ago that she wasn't faking, but still he only half believed in Hek, the way a little kid half believes in Santa Claus. But here Hek was, spooky and beautiful and overwhelming. If Dougie had suddenly found himself at Santa's North Pole workshop, he wouldn't have been more surprised.

Dougie had listened to Varloo, had visited caves with his mom, had read about prehistoric people and even some modern-day people who lived in caves. But none of that prepared him for the reality of this place, a whole world underground. And the first thing that wowed him was how clean everything was. Except that the air felt damp and there was no daylight, it wasn't Dougie's idea of a cave at all.

The first room, the one at the bottom of the staircase, made him think of the entry hall in a mansion. The floor, walls, and ceiling were made of a polished cream-colored stone that was smooth, shiny, and slick, as if it had just been scrubbed. On the walls were intricate patterns, spiral shapes of all sizes that reminded Dougie of seashells. But that didn't make sense. They were a hundred miles from the ocean. Then he remembered: These limestone caves were sometimes full of fossils. The patterns in the walls were made from thousands of them.

That Dougie could see the patterns at all amazed him too. He searched for a light source and finally found it: a row of tiny lanterns. Two tunnels led away from this entrance room, and Dougie could see that the lanterns continued along them too. The light they gave off was soft, dimmer than moonlight. Once his eyes adjusted, though, he could see pretty well.

"What is the meaning of this?" said a deep voice. "What is the meaning . . . of him? Where are the searchers?"

Dougie had been so busy looking at the scenery he had not seen the figures standing in the shadows near the far wall of the entry room. Now he counted ten. So these were the Druids and the principal Bard. Varloo had filled him in on the welcoming ceremony, and they were the ones who were invited. They didn't look much different from the searchers he had already seen on the Surface. Same short, roly-poly bodies. Same churchy robes. The man who spoke was the smallest of all of them and probably the roundest too. His voice was powerful. This must be the head Druid, the one temporarily buried by the backhoe. Geber was his name. He looked like he had recovered just fine.

"The searchers were safe when we left them," Varloo said in a strong, clear voice. "My companion is what he appears to be, an Extro boy, age eleven years. He does come in peace and in tolerance of our ways. He has been my helper on the Surface, just as Lugh was Drasil's helper."

"Lugh?" Dougie looked at Varloo. "Who's Lugh?"

"'Twas Asa Gonner's Hekian name," Varloo whispered.

"Silence!" said the man with the deep voice.

"Sorry," Dougie said.

He wasn't supposed to say anything till they were alone with her mother. But he was so bad at keeping quiet. Varloo knows that as well as any-body, he thought.

There was a bunch of ritual mumbo jumbo that was supposed to happen at this ceremony, Varloo had told him. It sounded a little like church to Dougie. But apparently his showing up had thrown a wrench in the works. Everybody looked pretty confused.

A woman stepped forward. She was almost pretty, and Dougie realized with surprise that that was because she resembled Varloo. It must be Persephone, her mother.

"You will come with me, Extro. And daughter," she said. She sounded bossy. It must run in the family.

"By what authority do you take them?" Geber asked.

"By the authority of the Ovate," she said.

The other Hekians looked at one another and whispered. Dougie was glad Varloo had told him about Ovates. Persephone seems to be pulling rank, he thought. But Geber's the head guy. What is going to happen to me? If I get to pick, I definitely want Mom.

"'Tis unprecedented," Geber said, but he didn't sound so sure of himself now.

185

"In our lifetime the appearance of an Extro boy in this hall also is unprecedented," said Persephone. "I ask your indulgence, Geber. I shall ascertain the nature of the boy's visit. Of his relationship to my daughter, the Spy. I will ascertain the position of the searchers. Of these things I shall sing to the Council entire on the coming sleep."

"What think the council members?" Geber turned to the others.

Most heads were nodding, but a couple of people raised their hands as if they were in school, wanting to be called on. Mom didn't wait to hear their questions. "Come along, daughter. You as well, Extro. We shall go to our dwelling place. I shall prepare tea."

Chapter Thirty-five

IT SEEMED TO TAKE the Hekians a few moments to recover from their surprise. In that time Dougie, Varloo, and her mom had left the hall and started down the left tunnel. Now, though, behind them, Dougie heard shouted questions.

"Is he a prisoner of the Ovate?"

"Geber, was this the wisest—?"

"Make haste, daughter. Quickly now, Extro," Persephone said. "They are a moody lot. I may not have you long."

Dougie wasn't sure if he was allowed to talk yet, so he didn't answer. He was busy looking around anyway. As they walked, he saw that other, smaller tunnels branched off. How big was it down here? He had never asked Varloo that.

Dougie figured they had gone a quarter mile when they came to a narrow stairway, also made of polished rock. Down, down, down they walked. Hadn't these people heard of escalators? Then, suddenly, the stairwell opened up, and they stepped out into another domed room.

Even in the fake moonlight this one was so vast, and so beautiful, Dougie stopped short with his mouth open.

"The Park," Varloo murmured. "There is nothing on the Surface like it."

Dougie noticed something else. The whole place seemed deserted.

"Where is everybody?" he asked.

"Asleep," Varloo said. "Remember? We keep the hours of the bats, awakening at the time you call dusk, going to sleep at the time you call dawn. The Druids only remained awake to welcome us."

Some welcome, Dougie thought.

Now the path wound among rock formations the way a trail winds through the woods. Dougie had read about the great caverns of America—Carlsbad in New Mexico, Crystal and Mammoth in Kentucky—but this chamber was larger and more beautiful than any he had ever heard of or seen in photographs.

He was glad he had been studying caves so he could name what he was seeing. Those massive bouquets of multicolored rock "flowers" dripping from the ceiling were helictites; the gigantic rock icicles were stalactites; rising to meet them from the floor were stalagmites, some as tall as trees. There was also flowstone, which looked like orange-striped drapes, something a giant with really bad taste would have in his castle. Dougie knew the strange shapes had been formed by water dripping for tens of thousands of years, and just as he thought that, he heard running water.

A few steps later they came to the most remarkable thing he had seen yet.

It was a bridge arching over a fast-flowing stream, a bridge made of white rock—quartz?—with railings of gold and silver. Real gold? Real silver? he wondered. But of course it was! This was gold country after all. All those years ago James Skerdoff was right. There was gold under Spook Hill, and the Hekians used it to make the railings of their bridges. For alchemists, it must have seemed like paradise. They didn't have to make precious metals. The metals were here for the taking.

Midway across the bridge Dougie heard a faint, low hum beneath the rush of water. He looked downstream and saw nothing, but when he looked the other way, he saw something in the distance that looked like a huge wheel. Still walking, he stared upstream and realized a few steps later that the view was clearer. Was the light getting brighter? Now he could tell that whatever the thing was, it was spinning like a Ferris wheel.

Dougie's face must have shown his confusion because Varloo whispered, "Electricity."

Dougie still didn't get it, but he hurried along, took a running step off the bridge, and almost tripped over a black wire that ran along the ground. It reminded Dougie of an extension cord, and then he understood the wheel. It must be hooked to a generator, like the turbines in the dam at Melones Reservoir, not far from Oak Hollow. These Hekians are almost as smart as we are, Dougie thought.

As they got close to the far wall of the chamber, Dougie could see where the path disappeared into a tunnel again. Then he noticed something else about the wall. White curtains were draped here and there, like doorways in an apartment building. Some of them had pictures of oak trees on them. Were these their houses?

Dougie didn't have to wonder long. Only a little way into the next tunnel they came to another curtain, this one edged in gold. Varloo's mother pushed the flap back and practically shoved Dougie inside.

"Home." Varloo sighed. "Thank Drake!"

Dougie didn't know what he was expecting, but after the splendor of the park and the silver and gold bridge, it wasn't this. Varloo's whole house was hardly bigger than a den for a hibernating bear, even if it was a whole lot brighter and tidier. The walls were smooth and white, with painted decorations like the pictures Dougie had seen of Egyptian tombs.

The whole place looked only about ten feet by ten feet, with a low ceiling. Dougie kept bumping his head.

"Sit thee down, Extro," said Varloo's mother. "We will be safe here, for now."

Dougie sat on a rock bench covered with moss. None too comfortable on his bruised tailbone. There was a second bench just like it on the opposite wall, and he realized these must be their beds as well as their couches. No wonder Varloo slept fine in the tree house; this bed felt . . . well, hard as a rock.

Chapter Thirty-six

DOUGIE DIDN'T LIKE any kind of tea, but all this explanation was taking so long he finally went ahead and drank it. Disgusting! Cough syrup minus the cherry flavoring. No wonder Varloo loved Kool-Aid.

Still, he felt a little better with tea in his belly. Dougie's brain was bewildered by lack of sleep, the sights of Hek, and the risk he was taking. Down here, he realized, anything could happen to him. That guy Geber might show up anytime and decide to blast him. Who would ever know? Then there were the thoughts of home that kept intruding. My poor parents, he thought for the millionth time. At least when Varloo was on her Mission, her mom knew where she was.

Anyway, the tea made his brain feel as if it might still be working. And maybe he could try some of those mushroom cake deals later. Varloo had said they weren't too bad. Dougie suspected he would need all the brainpower he could dredge up.

Dougie had been too tired to pay close attention to Varloo's telling her mom about her Mission, the searchers, almost being blasted. It was a familiar story. But now he heard her say, ". . . an Extro Tenet about harming certain bats."

Good, he thought. You're getting to the point. A moment later he realized Varloo had stopped talking, and both she and her mother were looking at him. Was he supposed to say something? He didn't know. He smiled, then remembered Varloo's mother wasn't likely to appreciate a smile. So he frowned instead.

"Indeed he is quite bright," Varloo told her mother. "Mayhap our teachings about the Extros are . . . out-of-date."

"There are others who think as you do," said her mother. "But this talk is for later. Tell me again about the decision of the Extros' Council."

"'Tis Dougie's plan," said Varloo. "I told you, Mother. As the Spy I have failed. I do admit it freely."

"Likewise that is for later, my dear. Extro"—she turned to Dougie—"tell me this plan. Begin with the role of the Extros' Council."

Dougie figured she must mean the planning commission. He explained it all as best he could, and surprisingly she seemed to understand at once.

"I see a problem," she said. "The Extros' Council will want proof that the bats do live here. Mayhap that will mean sending Extros to investigate. Extros like the one who caused the cave-in. 'Tis likely they may be as damaging as LeRoy Shaeffer's shelters."

"I know that," said Dougie. "But that's what's so great about my plan. I collect the evidence—bring back the bat—myself. No scientists necessary."

"Aye," said Persephone thoughtfully. "Aye, there is a chance. But if that be our intent, we must act this very sleep. Geber will keep to our agreement—if he can. But the other Druids may press him. Even as an Ovate I cannot guarantee your safety for long."

Dougie took a deep breath to steady his pounding heart.

"Now let us eat," said Persephone. "And then let us muster our strength by obtaining some rest. We shall move as soon as we are able. At the time of the awakening."

Chapter Thirty-seven

JUDAH THOUGHT HIS PARENTS made much too big a fuss when Dougie wasn't in his bed Thursday morning. In fact he felt a lot worse about losing Fortuna than he did about losing Dougie. Dougie was just in the woods somewhere. Like on Sunday mornings.

The first police officer who came to the house even agreed with Judah, more or less. He told Mom and Dad they wouldn't start a full-on search for a kid Dougie's age until he had been gone forty-eight hours.

"Most of the time these runaways come on home, dragging their tails behind them," the officer said.

"But he's not a runaway," Mom had argued.

"Mark my words, ma'am, he'll be back. But we'll keep an eye out. If any of our patrol cars see him, we'll be in touch."

Now it was Friday noon. And even Judah was worried. His brother had been gone more than a day. Mom and Dad were frantic. They wanted to go out looking themselves, but the officer who came today said it was better to stay home in case Dougie came back or someone called with information.

Mom hadn't slept much that night, so she was lying down. Dad was making phone calls. It seemed to Judah he had been forgotten. No one even cared if he went to school, so he didn't. Now there was nothing to do.

Maybe I should look for Dougie myself, Judah thought. But he immediately dismissed the idea. Hadn't it been bad enough going out to the tree house Wednesday night? The woods were like acre upon acre of creepy zone.

On the other hand, Judah argued with himself, Mom and Dad would make a big to-do over the person who found Dougie. If that were me, I'd be the family hero. Judah liked that idea. Then he thought of Kit Carson. I'd be tracking Dougie. Just like Kit used to track the enemy. I could wear thick socks under my sneakers. And Levi's. And a long-sleeved shirt. My Niners hat. Nothing creepy could get near my skin that way.

Twenty minutes later Judah was trotting along the trail toward the overlook. He had never been out here, but he knew from Mom and Dad that the trail was pretty well marked, and eventually it went to a creek. He figured if he moved fast, he'd beat out the snakes and spiders, not to mention relatives of snakes and spiders. But running in all these clothes was pretty sweaty work.

There was no sign of Dougie so far. But when he looked for Fortuna on Wednesday, he hadn't known what kind of sign he was looking for either. He missed his cat. He never had found her. But he had found some fur. Some clue would show up this time too.

Up the hill he ran. Judah could hear somethi overhead. It sounded like the *thuppa-thupp* helicopter, but he couldn't see anything the trees. When finally he got to the top he looked back toward town and s four-by-four on a fire road below hir

Who else is out here? he wonder wouldn't have started their search remembered the county scientists. were doing some kind of study today. She hoped maybe they'd spo

Judah had good wind. He ran walked the down, not wanting ankle with the play-offs so clos when he felt it. Something gooey had attached itself to the sole of his shoe. He winced. What horrible, creepy thing had he squished? Disgusted in anticipation, he looked at his foot.

Eeeeeyew—something pink like bloody flesh . . . wrinkled and sticky and . . .

Wait a minute. It was bubble gum. Bubble gum like he chewed himself. Bubble gum like his brother, Dougie, chewed too.

Chapter Thirty-eight

DOUGIE HADN'T THOUGHT much of the mushroom cakes, but probably they were healthier than yesterday's diet, the Oreo, water, and bubble-gum diet. Then, even on a rock bed, he had slept a while. He dreamed three-toed pill bugs with guns were chasing him through an anthill. It was a terrible dream. Now, after his second long walk with Varloo and her mom, he was standing in still another large chamber.

"Holy guacamole!" he breathed.

In contrast with the gleaming cleanliness of every other place in Hek, this room was stinky, the floors slick and goopy, the walls and ceiling constantly shimmering and shifting as though they were alive. A shadow swooped overhead, and in spite of himself Dougie shuddered. "Are those . . . are they all—"

"Bats," said Varloo, wrinkling her nose because of the ammonia smell. "This is the farm."

"You mean you eat bats?"

"By Drake, no!" Varloo said. "Have I not explained? 'Tis the guano we want."

"Guano?" Oh, right. Bat poop. Dougie picked up each foot and looked at the soles of his shoes. Yuck!

"'Tis foolish to be squeamish, Extro. We must do what we must do to prosper. 'Tis no different on the Surface."

Before they had left to walk here, Persephone had been anxious about what the average Hekian might do if he found out there was an Extro around. Extros were not exactly popular in Hek. Most people were still asleep, but to be safe, she had disguised him in one of the heavy robes. With its hood they had covered his Raiders cap. Then she told him to stoop so he wouldn't attract attention. That was easy enough. When he stood straight, he risked conking his head. It was weird to feel like a giant. He was just a normal-size kid, wasn't he?

In this strange place he didn't know who he was.

"The farmer should be harvesting by now, but his sloth is well known," Persephone said. "For years Geber has sought to have him assigned to sentry duty, but Maria, the Druid, is his step-mother, and she does not permit it. However, today his sloth does give us advantage."

Persephone removed something from the pocket of her robes. It looked like a sock stuffed with dirt. "Which do you prefer?" she asked Dougie.

"Prefer?"

"She means, which type of bat do you wish to take with you?" Varloo explained.

Dougie thought hard. What had that article in the newspaper said about bats? Then he remembered: "The Mexican ones."

"What is 'Mexican'?" Persephone asked.

"Oh, yeah. That's no help. Uh . . ." He thought some more. "Something about tails?" he said. "Is there a kind that has a funny tail?"

Persephone smiled. "Aye. I know which are these. The ones with the long tails that do come in the season of the Flood; you do call it spring, I believe. They have sweet faces, these bats. The Ancestors compared them with the creatures called dogs."

"Dogs, yeah," Dougie said. "But what's the sock—" He didn't have to finish the question. Varloo's mom swung it around twice and hurled it at some bats hanging a few feet away.

"Your pardons I do beg!" she called as twenty or thirty, rudely awakened, flew at the sock thing, making *eep* noises. A moment later it fell back to earth. Attached to it was one very angry, wiggly bat.

"We mean no harm," Varloo said as she popped what looked like a cup over it and slid a lid underneath. Then she flipped the cup over, pressed the perforated lid firmly into place, and held the whole thing out to Dougie. "Your bat," she said. "Treat her well."

Dougie really, really did not want to take it, but he swallowed hard and did. The poor little thing was about six inches long and weighed practically nothing. She was furry all over, and her face had a flat nose that was a little like a bulldog's, Dougie thought. She was also mad and fluttering wildly; Dougie felt bad for her.

"Put her beneath your robe," Varloo said. "That should calm her down."

Dougie did as he was told. He could feel the poor trapped creature flapping against him, and the sensation made his skin crawl. But soon, as Varloo had predicted, the bat was still. Maybe she likes me, Dougie thought.

Persephone had been looking about the chamber, and now she said anxiously, "O my Drake, *no!*" Dougie was afraid the Druids had come for him, but he saw no one. Then he realized the bats were becoming restless. Apparently the sock thing had set off a chain reaction.

"You are out of practice," Varloo said.

"Aye," said her mother. "'Twas none too gently thrown. I fear I have aroused a stampede. But there should be no dire effects—beyond the farmer's wrath. I do have more now to explain to the Druids, however. 'Tis another verse for my Song."

By this time the bats were going crazy. In an instant, as if by magic, they vanished from the walls and ceilings while the smelly air became windy with their beating wings. Like a living whirlwind, they wheeled round and round the chamber until, as one, they swept through a large opening overhead.

"Fare thee well!" Varloo called after them. Then, abruptly, all was silent.

Chapter Thirty-nine

JUDAH WAS MAKING HIS WAY across the dead tree when about three zillion bats swooped right at him and almost knocked him into the creek. He heard the flapping first, then felt a gust of air and looked up to see them coming for him. As the first ones whooshed by, he squeezed his eyes shut and covered up his hair so none would get tangled in it.

"Our Father . . ." He began and was halfway through the Lord's Prayer before he realized the air was quiet again. The bats were gone. They hadn't hurt him. God must have been listening. I'm glad I don't cut church every week like Dougie, he thought.

Judah was pretty sure he was on the right track. He had stepped on another piece of chewed bubble gum just before he jumped up on the tree trunk. Now he scraped his sneakers on a rock to get the mud off. Where to next?

Walking in the woods had given Judah plenty of time to think about how life would be without Dougie. Who would he fight with? Who would he tease when the awesome 49ers won and the misfit

Raiders lost? It might get a little boring actually. By now Judah wasn't so interested in being a hero. He mostly wanted to make sure his brother was okay.

But he didn't see a way through the bushes and trees on this side of the creek. And out here was the last place he wanted to be at night—especially after all those bats. Judah looked around him, trying to decide what to do next.

Then he heard something. A familiar and welcome sound. A cat's insistent meow.

"Fortuna?"

There she was, or at least there was her tail, disappearing under a bush.

"Fortuna!"

But the darned cat didn't come. She ran the other way.

"Oh, no, you don't," said Judah. "I'm not letting you go this time." And he ran after her, first through a narrow opening in the brush, where he almost got her by the scruff of the neck, and then up the steep hillside beyond.

Who knew his cat was such a track star? She ran and ran uphill, not stopping to rest even once. Judah was breathless by the time she finally sat down alongside a big white boulder resting, like a landmark, on the hillside.

Fortuna washed her face, then looked at Judah

and meowed her loud meow. Judah walked all around the rock but couldn't see anything unusual about it. Well, wait—there was a little hole, maybe big enough for a rabbit, at the base of the rock. But what did a rabbit hole have to do with anything?

Mustering every ounce of bravery he had, Judah reached a little way into the hole—and felt something soft and sticky and awful, a little wad of something exactly like . . . chewed bubble gum.

Chapter Forty

THIS WAS IT. Dougie had been so happy thinking about getting out of here, going home, being safe and secure and himself again in his own world, he had neglected to think about what it would be like to leave Varloo. His friend. Leave her forever.

But Varloo seemed to be thinking about something else entirely. "My necklace."

"What?" Dougie had expected something a little more . . . well, friendly.

"My necklace, emblem of the Spy," she said. They were standing in the domed fossil hall at the entrance to Hek. A crowd of Hekians was watching.

The bat stampede had attracted so much attention that there had been no way to keep Dougie a secret anymore. Persephone had acted every bit the high and mighty Ovate, ordering everyone away. But Dougie could see how her hands trembled as she hustled them here. It had been a long and scary walk.

Now she stood next to Dougie and Varloo with her arms folded and a stern expression on her face, daring anybody to mess with her. Geber was expected at any moment. Dougie didn't know whether that was good or bad. Geber had backed Persephone up the first time, but she said the Druids were a moody bunch. Would he have changed his mind by now? And if he had, what did that mean to Dougie?

Dougie hated to leave Varloo. But he wanted to get out of here, and he was beginning to think it had better be soon. These roly-poly Hekians did not look friendly.

"We have had so much to say to each other, so much to plan," Varloo was saying, "I did forget the necklace. I have lost it. 'Tis precious, a traditional symbol of the Spy."

Dougie slipped his fingers underneath the Raiders cap and scratched his head. "So you're saying if I find it, I should return it? Like how? Put it in the mail?"

Varloo smiled, then turned her head quickly so no Hekian would see. "Slip it beneath the Portal rock," she whispered.

Persephone stepped between them and said, "I shall pull the lever myself. I had thought to wait for the Druids' approval, but now do I see 'twill be safer for you to leave at once."

"It does violate the Tenet, Mother!" Varloo looked anxious.

"Aye. Another thing I must needs explain. My Song does grow ever more interesting." The lever was behind Persephone. Before the crowd realized what she was doing, she had reached it and pulled. The staircase began its whirring descent, causing an outcry among the people watching. Dougie heard that word *Tenet* over and over.

"Well . . ." Dougie felt embarrassed as, waiting for the staircase, he looked down into Varloo's oversize blue eyes. "I guess I'm outta here."

But before Varloo could reply, two Hekians moved forward, and somebody shouted, "Seize them!"

"Go!" Persephone said urgently.

Dougie didn't need to be told twice. The stairs had not yet reached the ground, but he jumped for them, pulled himself up, and half climbed, half ran for the top. The bat didn't like the jiggling and started flapping against Dougie's rib cage, but he ignored it and kept going. Halfway up he paused for breath and looked back. Dougie could have sworn Varloo's eyes had been dry a minute ago, but now her face was damp with tears.

"Fare thee well, Dougie! And thank you!" she called, and flashed him a sad smile. With that, the crowd of Hekians surrounded her.

Seconds later Dougie crawled into the moonlight. His world was blurred by the tears in his eyes.

Chapter Forty-one

JUDAH JUMPED ABOUT A MILE and a half when his lost brother crawled out from under the big rock. Not only did he appear from nowhere, but he was wearing the weirdest clothes Judah had ever seen. They looked like bathrobes stacked on top of each other. The only normal thing was the Raiders cap.

"Where did you come from?" Judah's voice was shaking.

Dougie looked pretty startled to see Judah too. But he recovered quickly and said, infuriatingly, "Never mind."

Now that Dougie was safe, Judah started to remember how much he hated him.

"I have been looking for you for the whole day . . . and Mom and Dad, they're basket cases, and there were those bats, and the police were at the house, I don't know what all, and you're wearing these clothes! The least you could do is tell me—"

Judah might have talked a lot longer, but a cat interrupted with a loud, whiny, complaining meow.

"Osi!" Dougie cried.

"Oh-see?" Judah said. "That's my cat. Fortuna."

"She is not your cat. Where did you get such a crazy idea? You don't even have a cat! Her name's Osi, and she belongs to—" Dougie shut his mouth. "Well, it doesn't matter who she belongs to. She isn't yours anyway."

"Look, troglodyte," Judah said, "since we've rescued you and everything, Fortuna and I are going home. You can come if you want, or you can stay here for all I care."

Dougie looked up as if he were planning to say something equally nasty, but he never got the chance. A loud *boom* echoed across the hillside, and something way faster than any insect zoomed past Judah's head.

Judah had no idea what the deal was, but when he saw the terrified look on Dougie's face, he got scared too.

A second later he heard a peculiar voice: "Remain where you be, Extros. Your time has come."

Chapter Forty-two

FROZEN WITH FEAR, Dougie peered into the twilight and, after a moment, spotted the small figure huddled beside the oak tree a few yards up the hill. At first, with his dull-colored robe, he looked like part of the tree trunk. Dougie doubted Judah even had seen him. Dougie kept staring and soon made out that Fen held what must be a blaster in his hands. So much for life and hope. He and Judah were as good as toast.

But then Dougie had an inspiration. What was it that had saved Hek in Drasil's Song? He didn't care what those Druids said. He knew it wasn't the spectacle.

Dougie took a deep breath. "Hey, Fen!" he shouted, his voice quavering. "Did you hear the one about the hamburgers who had a baby girl?"

"You're telling jokes?" Judah hissed.

"Whatever I say," Dougie whispered, "laugh your head off."

"Extros." The voice spoke again. "You do waste

your breath with your buffoonery."

"They named her Patty!" Dougie hollered. Then he elbowed his brother and commanded, "Laugh!" while he himself doubled over shouting "Ha-ha-ha!" and trying to smile.

"What?" Judah must have thought he'd lost his mind.

"Hey, short stuff!" Dougie yelled again, and this time his voice was steadier. "What do you call a piece of wood with nothing to do? Board! Get it? B-O-R-E-D?"

Dougie was whooping, but Judah continued to stand there looking blank. "Think of the Three Stooges," Dougie gasped between ha's. "Think of Animaniacs—ha-ha-ha—anything, just laugh!"

Judah managed a weak, puzzled titter. "Not good enough!" Dougie said, working up to a big guffaw himself, and he poked his brother in his most ticklish spot, which at least made him spit out a few grunts.

Dougie looked again to where the Hekian stood. The blaster was still aimed. "Hee-hee-hee!" Dougie cried desperately, and Judah, getting into the spirit, echoed him.

"Fare thee well, Extro," called the voice. Then *boom,* there was another report and a startled

Mreeeow! from behind the rock. For a terrible moment Dougie thought Osi had been hit, but another, smaller *mew* told him the cat was okay. He was so relieved he laughed for real.

"Okay." Dougie panted. "I think we got a few seconds before he reloads. Don't stop laughing—har-har-har—but get ready to run like crazy for that little pine tree down there. They can't shoot what they can't see."

"What about my cat?" Judah asked. Then he snickered for good measure.

"She's not yours! And thanks for reminding me." Dougie couldn't just leave her with Fen blasting everything in sight. Quickly Dougie scooped Osi up, then knelt and pushed her under the rock. He hoped the stairs were still in place. Otherwise it was a pretty good drop. But cats always land on their feet, right?

"Come on, bro," Dougie said, then grabbed Judah's hand and took off running.

The robe and the bat trap slowed Dougie down, and his brother was faster anyway. Soon Judah had let go of his hand and was way out in front. When Dougie looked back over his shoulder, he took a wrong step and—wham! He tripped over the hem of the robe and sprawled flat on the hillside.

"Keep going!" he shouted to Judah, but Judah turned back and pulled him to his feet. Dougie fumbled with the robe and finally managed to slip it off, but in the process he dropped the precious bat. "Run!" he told his brother, while he frantically shook the heavy fabric and freed the trap. Then he was off again down the hill.

Judah was almost to the tree, almost safe, when Dougie heard another boom and saw him stumble.

"Judah!" Dougie called. His brother didn't move. Had he been blasted? If he's dead, it's my fault, Dougie thought. He came out looking for me. He stopped to help me up. I as good as killed him.

Dougie threw himself down by the body of his brother. "Oh, Judah," he gasped, "I'm so sorry!" Dougie could feel the tears on his cheek.

"Well, you don't have to blubber about it," Judah said. "I just tripped. Come on." Dougie had never in his life expected to be glad to hear that pipsqueak voice. But he sure was glad now. Together they sprang to their feet, and a second later they were both behind the tree.

"Can I stop laughing yet?" Judah whispered.

"Yes, you can stop laughing!" Wouldn't his brother ever understand anything? "Come on. I think we're still in range. We've gotta get to the creek."

Together they ran the rest of the way down the hill as if their lives depended on it, but no more booms blasted the hillside. Had Fen given up? Dougie wondered.

Breathing hard, the brothers reached the cover of the thicket by Stick Creek and squeezed through the opening in the brush. "Want to rest?" Dougie asked. "I think we're safe here."

"Hunh-unh." Judah shook his head. "I just want to go home."

"Me too."

They crossed the creek and started running up the path to the overlook, but Dougie soon slowed to a walk. "I'm sorry," he told Judah. "I'm just so exhausted. You wouldn't believe—"

"Who was that guy anyway? Why was he shooting at us? And how come you shoved my cat under a rock?" Judah seemed to have a zillion questions, and they all spewed out. Dougie couldn't blame him. It *would* seem pretty weird if you didn't know what was going on.

Come to think of it, it seemed pretty weird even if you did know what was going on: They were being shot at by a Druid from a secret civilization Dougie was going to save when he gave his mom the wiggling bat he was clutching by his side. The cat was sacred and being returned to its rightful owner, who lived under the rock.

Dougie didn't have to worry about keeping this secret. It was too weird to tell. Nobody would ever believe it.

"Okay, Dougie," Judah said after they had walked a little farther in silence. "You aren't going to tell me anything about where you were. Fine. Then I'll just tell Mom and Dad what I saw. The guy shooting at us. Everything."

"You can't do that," Dougie said.

"Hide and watch," said Judah.

Dougie thought fast. "What if I agree to tell everybody you are a hero? That you really did rescue me? Even though you had nothing to do with it and, as a matter of fact, I saved your life."

They walked a few steps in silence as Judah seemed to consider. "Okay," he said. "It's a deal. But I do have one question."

Dougie thought maybe he could make something up. "Go ahead, slimebucket."

"Well," said Judah, "what I want to know is this, toadbreath. Where'd you learn such terrible jokes?"

"Terrible? I didn't think they were so terrible!"

"They were, without a doubt, the worst jokes

218

I ever heard. Even babies know better jokes than that."

"Well, they worked, didn't they? If I hadn't told those jokes, we'd be—"

The two boys crested the overlook and saw their house below them. The sight shut them both up—for about a second and a half. Then they started arguing again and didn't stop until they reached the backyard and their tearful mom and dad came running out to welcome them back home.

Chapter Forty-three

DRAMATIC REVELATIONS HALT HOUSING PROJECT

Commission seeks U.S. protection for hidden cavern

by Chris Hopkins

Oak Hollow—Over loud protests from developer LeRoy Shaeffer, planning commissioners Wednesday night voted to deny his permit to build Collina Fantastica, a 1,000-home development on an isolated hillside east of town.

Further, commissioners expressed their intention of seeking federal protection for the land, which experts say conceals a cavern that is home to a significant colony of Mexican free-tailed bats and possibly to other ecologically significant creatures as well.

"Well, naturally we're tickled pink," said Doria Capehart of the Foothill Defense Fund (FDF), which had opposed the housing project. "The somewhat unusual circumstances surrounding this case have focused attention on the plight of bats and the need to protect our region's unique limestone caverns from human interlopers."

Shaeffer refused to speak to reporters after the

decision. However, he did reiterate his belief that "houses for people are more important than caves for bats" and "once again the government has prevented an upstanding citizen from making a decent living."

Wednesday's unanimous vote is the final chapter in a saga that began in May, when Shaeffer announced his plans. Environmentalists moved quickly to block the development.

Then, on May 26, two days after the commission had voted to require an environmental study of the project's impacts, a county team making a survey of the site witnessed what one called a wondrous sight: thousands of bats emerging all at once from a previously unknown fissure in the seldom-visited hillside. (See photo at right.)

Biologists had long suspected a bat colony lived in the region but were stunned by the enormousness of this one. "Its size alone makes it a significant contributor to the ecological balance of the foothills," says the county's environmental report.

The story took a bizarre turn that night when the presence of the bats was confirmed by Douglas Minners, age 11. Minners had disappeared from his home 36 hours before, and police were readying to mount a search. But as it happened, Minners's brother, Judah, age 10, had conducted his own unauthorized search, and he brought the lost boy home. At the time of his return Douglas was carrying on his person a healthy, mature female bat confined in a trap.

Coincidentally, Douglas is the son of Cynthia

Minners, lawyer for the Foothill Defense Fund.

Douglas Minners's bat was duly turned over to wildlife authorities, who displayed it several days later at a meeting of the planning commission. Several commissioners shrieked when Cynthia Minners removed the drape from the bat's cage, and one audience member had to leave the room.

When order was restored, Cynthia Minners explained that the bat's species had been positively identified. She said further that allowing the housing project to go forward would invite a costly lawsuit the county certainly would lose. The bat was subsequently released, but the fate of LeRoy Shaeffer's development was sealed.

As for Douglas Minners, he told authorities he got lost while doing research on caves for a school project. In the course of his research, he told police, he captured the bat and decided to bring her back for his teacher.

"I needed the extra credit," he said.

The day after his return both Douglas and his brother were admitted to Oak Hollow Hospital, suffering from severe cases of poison oak.

Chapter Forty-four

WHEN SUZY SHAEFFER FOUND out Dougie and Judah Minners got to spend a whole day and night in the hospital for poison oak, she felt cheated.

On the same day they had met up with poison oak bushes, she had met up with a new horse that bucked her off and broke her ankle. But all she got out of the deal was the emergency room and a walking cast. There wasn't even time for her friends to come by and give her stuffed animals.

Suzy changed her mind about feeling cheated, though, when she visited Dougie and Judah in the hospital. Judah looked bad, but Dougie looked worse, as bumpy and puffed up as the blowfish picture in her online encyclopedia.

"I'll come visit when you get home," she had told Dougie. "I think my bike's still in your garage."

Dougie only nodded. Talking made his face itch.

Two days later Suzy's parents came to her bedroom with the biggest wrapped-up present Suzy had ever seen. Inside was a guitar.

Suzy was thrilled.

"Not so fast," said her dad. "There're three con-ditions."

"Should've known," Suzy said. "What?"

The deal was this: (1) Suzy would give up horse-back riding lessons; (2) Suzy would take up guitar lessons; (3) Suzy would be a lot safer.

Not for nothing was Suzy the daughter of a lawyer. She made a counteroffer: (1) I will give up horseback riding lessons; (2) I will take up guitar lessons; (3) You will give me a mountain bike.

Negotiations among the interested parties yielded an agreement, provided Condition No. 4 was also met: Suzy would always always always wear a helmet.

Chapter Forty-five

DOUGIE NEEDED ONE MORE thing and he'd be ready for the hike to Spook Hill.

Bubble gum.

It was a long way, and he hadn't stolen any in quite a while.

Judah was at baseball practice, as usual. So Dougie didn't need to be sneaky. He just marched into Judah's room.

"Hi, Kitty," he said to the new goldfish. Was he imagining things, or did it flip its tail in response? Maybe fish, like cat, was an easy language to learn.

Kitty lived in a bowl on top of Judah's dresser. Judah had been so sad about losing Osi that even Dougie felt bad. So he had gone to the pet store and gotten him a goldfish. It wasn't the same, but with his mom's allergies, it was the best he could do.

Judah's bubble gum—not to mention all his other "secret" stuff—was kept with his underwear in the top drawer. Dougie pulled the drawer open . . . and stared.

"Holy guacamole!" There, on top of Judah's usual stash, lay Varloo's gold necklace.

With the necklace and the newspaper clipping in his backpack, Dougie hiked out to Spook Hill, chewing and blowing bubbles all the way. When he got to the Portal rock, he felt a surge of something he hadn't expected. Sadness. He really missed Varloo. He was pretty sure he'd never have another friend like her. He hoped she was okay. He hoped those moody Druids hadn't done anything crazy.

What Dougie did next was probably stupid. She would never appreciate how much it meant. Still, she had lost her hat in the creek, hadn't she? And they never got around to finding her a new one.

He did it quick so he couldn't think twice: Take off Raiders cap, stuff clipping and necklace inside, rubber band it all together, push it under rock.

There. G'bye, James Jett. Hope you like it, Varloo. Maybe I'll bring her some Oreos next time.

There was no point hanging around now. So Dougie started the walk home to meet Suzy. She was bringing her guitar over so he could try it out. She said the lessons were really fun, and she didn't mind practicing.

Dougie thought he might ask for a guitar for his birthday. Lately he had had a whole bunch of ideas for songs he wanted to write.

Chapter Forty-six

I sing the virtue of friendship,
No bound'ries does it know,
No limitations of nature,
No constraints laid by fear.
I sing the virtue of friendship,
Which o'ercomes space and time
Tenacious, tolerant, gen'rous
True hero of my Song.

From the *Story of Hek*,
the *Song of Varloo*

"**V**ARLOO! COME QUICKLY. Something wonderful!"

Varloo had been taking her turn at the fishery when her grandmother approached. Osi was weaving her way around Varloo's legs, meowing loudly in hopes of getting a taste. Osi had never been so friendly as now, when Varloo worked at the fishery.

"Please, Thor, may Varloo not come with me for a moment?" Brigid asked. "'Tis a miracle. Even Geber does say so."

"She is not of much Hekly use here," Thor said. "Never did anyone clean fish so awkwardly."

Brigid sucked in a breath but replied only,

"Thank you, Thor. Come, Varloo. Bring the cat if you wish, but make haste!"

"Thor is awful!" Varloo whispered as she removed her apron and wiped her hands. "So disrespectful! You would think I was an ordinary—"

"Varloo?"

Varloo sighed. "Aye, Grandmother. Come along, Osi."

Indeed Varloo knew she was fortunate to have work, fortunate not to be confined to her dwelling place—or worse. For a moment immediately after the helper had ascended the staircase, Varloo had thought her own people might do her injury. They were that angry at the presence of an Extro in Hek. But then the sacred cat had come prancing down the forbidden staircase, appearing as if by magic and diverting the crowd's attention. Geber arrived shortly after. He believed that the cat was an omen, a good one. Varloo and Persephone would have a very interesting Song to sing, he said. The Council awaited their Song eagerly. When it had been sung entire, the Council would make a decision about whether to punish the Spy.

Later on that same sleep the searchers had returned. Fen was in the custody of Maria and Brigid. The two women had been delayed first by the presence of Extros near the Portal rock and then by the necessity of capturing and overpowering Fen. It seemed he had been attempting to blast two Extro boys who were running down the hillside.

Two boys? Not one? Varloo had not understood. But Fen had not succeeded in harming anyone. That much the searchers could tell her for certain.

Now, walking with her grandmother, Varloo wondered what was this latest news. Where were they going?

As the two approached the Portal hall, Varloo saw that Geber and Persephone waited there. She saw something else as well. On the floor lay a black and silver bundle. From its position it seemed to have dropped directly from the trapdoor in the rock.

"From the Extro," Persephone said. "I do recognize—"

"—his hat," said Varloo. She felt tears well in her eyes.

"We did not move it," said Geber. "We thought we should leave that for you. However, we could not help but, uh—"

"Peek," said Brigid.

Varloo knelt by the bundle and saw what the others had seen when they did peek. Wrapped inside the Raiders cap was the gold necklace of the Spy. And there was, besides, a piece of paper cut from the Extros' chronicle. Only the Ovate could read, of course. Varloo handed the paper to her mother.

Persephone studied it. "'Twill take time for me to decipher it," she said at last. "But the title I do understand. It says there are to be no shelters."

Geber looked pleased. "It would seem, then, that the plan of the Extro helper did meet its purpose," he said. "I cannot speak for the Council. Yet I do not doubt their decision. Neither you nor your mother will be punished for your conduct, Varloo. Indeed you have served us well."

Varloo hid her face behind the Raiders cap. She did not want them to see her smile. When she had recovered herself, she put the cap on her head and said, to the puzzlement of all who heard her, "Pride and poise."

A Note from the Author

*T*he *Spy Wore Shades* is a work of fantasy.

Even with the aid of the alchemical *secrets* contained in the Emerald Tablet (an actual book dating from around the first century A.D. and ascribed to a god the Greeks called Hermes and the Egyptians called Thoth), it is unlikely that a sixteenth-century band of English exiles could have survived life underground. The obstacles they would have faced—principally the difficulty in raising or finding adequate food—would have been too much for their technology to overcome.

However, there are many places in which the story of Dougie and Varloo does intersect with both historical and natural fact.

The Oakland Raiders, for example, really did win a spectacular 24–23 come-from-behind victory against the New York Jets on October 24, 1999. The details are as described in Chapter 1.

The life and times of the dashing English privateer, explorer, and naval hero Francis Drake are outlined accurately in the fictitious *Frank's Encyclopedia of Legend and Lore*. As anyone who has completed fourth grade in California knows, Drake did land somewhere on its northern coast in June 1579. Historians believe there may have been a second ship as well. That ship, however, would have been of Spanish, not English, origin—captured by Drake and his men in the course of their long and eventful journey. The existence of a band of Druid exiles under Drake's protection is, of course, my own invention.

Druidism itself, however, is real. Not a lot is known about it because the Druids, like my Hekians, kept no written records but preserved orally their beliefs and their history. Most of the other details about Druids, including their veneration of oak trees and their division into classes called Bards, Ovates, and Druids, are believed to be accurate.

By A.D. 1000, Druidism had given way to Christianity in most of Europe, but there may have been isolated groups that kept it alive after that. Had one of these groups been discovered in England during the tumultuous sixteenth century, it is quite likely that its leader would have been burned for heresy. The eighteenth century saw a resurgence of interest in Druidism, and there are today practicing adherents of it.

Many of the Hekian names—Uther, Brigid, and Lugh, for example—are taken from Druidic gods. The names Maria, Geber, and Kalvis belonged to significant figures in the history of alchemy, which is also described briefly in the convenient *Frank's.*

As for the bats, the Mexican free-tailed species does migrate north to roost in huge maternity colonies in the southwestern United States, possibly ranging as far as Calaveras County, California. Bats are very delicate and wonderful creatures, and they should never be harmed or captured. Dougie, you will recall, traps one only because he believes it's the sole way to save Hek.

The Hekians' clever and extensive use of bat guano is also based in fact. A component of it, sodium nitrate, was studied and used by the historical alchemists, is a key ingredient in gunpowder, and has medicinal uses. Guano makes good fertilizer too.

(If you're interested in more information about bats, and bat guano, a great organization to contact is Bat Conservation International, P.O. Box 162603, Austin, TX 78716. Its website is www. batcon.org.)

Bats are not the only animals that live in caves. There is an entire branch of biology, speleobiology, concerned with the unusual creatures that have adapted to life underground. Fish, salamanders, and many insects are among them.

The town of Oak Hollow is invented, but Calaveras County, home of Mark Twain's celebrated jumping frog, is a real place with real limestone caverns, many of them open to the public. My knowledge of Calaveras County, historic and present-day, comes from having lived nearby in Sonora for sixteen years. During some of that time, I was a newspaper reporter, covering too many planning commission debates over too many subdivisions.

When Suzy Shaeffer tells Dougie's dad, "You can't have truth without facts," she is only partly right. Facts are an element of truth, surely, but there is also the truth that goes beyond them. To my mind, the friendship between Dougie Minners and Varloo exemplifies that truth.

Oh—and Suzy? If you're listening? Bats don't get tangled up in people's hair. It's an old husbands' tale.